★ **FOR THE TRIBE**
who raised him, Abel was a source of pride
—and fear.

★ For the beautiful white woman who
seduced him, he was a sexual plaything that
became an obsession.

★ For the America that used him and
then destroyed him, he was a question that
could not be answered . . .

HOUSE MADE OF DAWN

HOUSE MADE OF DAWN

By

N. Scott Momaday

PERENNIAL LIBRARY
Harper & Row, Publishers
New York, Hagerstown, San Francisco, London

The author gratefully acknowledges the *Southern Review*, the *New Mexico Quarterly*, and *The Reporter*, in which excerpts of this book first appeared.

First PERENNIAL LIBRARY edition published 1977

ISBN: 0-06-080421-1

81 10 9 8 7 6 5

For Gaye

❀ PROLOGUE ❀

Dypaloh. There was a house made of dawn. It was made of pollen and of rain, and the land was very old and everlasting. There were many colors on the hills, and the plain was bright with different-colored clays and sands. Red and blue and spotted horses grazed in the plain, and there was a dark wilderness on the mountains beyond. The land was still and strong. It was beautiful all around.

Abel was running. He was alone and running, hard at first, heavily, but then easily and well. The road curved out in front of him and rose away in the distance. He could not see the town. The valley was gray with rain, and snow lay out upon the dunes. It was dawn. The first light had been deep and vague in the mist, and then the sun flashed and a great yellow glare fell under the cloud. The road verged upon clusters of juniper and mesquite, and he could see the black angles and twists of wood beneath the hard white crust; there was a shine and glitter on the ice. He was running, running. He could see the horses in the fields and the crooked line of the river below.

For a time the sun was whole beneath the cloud; then it rose into eclipse, and a dark and certain shadow came upon the land. And Abel was running. He was naked to the waist, and his arms and shoulders had been marked with burnt wood and ashes. The cold rain slanted down upon him and left his skin mottled and streaked. The road curved out and lay into the bank of rain beyond, and Abel was running. Against the winter sky and the long, light landscape of the valley at dawn, he seemed almost to be standing still, very little and alone.

7

1

THE LONGHAIR

Walatowa
Cañon de San Diego, 1945

JULY 20

The river lies in a valley of hills and fields. The north end of the valley is narrow, and the river runs down from the mountains through a canyon. The sun strikes the canyon floor only a few hours each day, and in winter the snow remains for a long time in the crevices of the walls. There is a town in the valley, and there are ruins of other towns in the canyon. In three directions from the town there are cultivated fields. Most of them lie to the west, across the river, on the slope of the plain. Now and then in winter, great angles of geese fly through the valley, and then the sky and the geese are the same color and the air is hard and damp and smoke rises from the houses of the town. The seasons lie hard upon the land. In summer the valley is hot, and birds come to the tamarack on the

river. The feathers of blue and yellow birds are prized
by the townsmen.

The fields are small and irregular, and from the west
mesa they seem an intricate patchwork of arbors and
gardens, too numerous for the town. The townsmen
work all summer in the fields. When the moon is full,
they work at night with ancient, handmade plows and
hoes, and if the weather is good and the water plentiful
they take a good harvest from the fields. They grow the
things that can be preserved easily: corn and chilies and
alfalfa. On the town side of the river there are a few
orchards and patches of melons and grapes and squash.
Every six or seven years there is a great harvest of
piñones far to the east of the town. That harvest, like
the deer in the mountains, is the gift of God.

It is hot in the end of July. The old man Francisco
drove a team of roan mares near the place where the
river bends around a cottonwood. The sun shone on the
sand and the river and the leaves of the tree, and waves
of heat shimmered from the stones. The colored stones
on the bank of the river were small and smooth, and
they rubbed together and cracked under the wagon
wheels. Once in a while one of the roan mares tossed its
head, and the commotion of its dark mane sent a
swarm of flies into the air. Downstream the brush grew
thick on a bar in the river, and there the old man saw
the reed. He turned the mares into the water and
stepped down on the sand. A sparrow hung from the
reed. It was upside down and its wings were partly
open and the feathers at the back of its head lay spread
in a tiny ruff. The eyes were neither open nor closed.
Francisco was disappointed, for he had wished for a
male mountain bluebird, breast feathers the pale color
of April skies or of turquoise, lake water. Or a summer
tanager: a prayer plume ought to be beautiful. He drew
the reed from the sand and cut loose the horsehair from
the sparrow's feet. The bird fell into the water and was
carried away in the current. He turned the reed in his
hands; it was smooth and nearly translucent, like the
spine of an eagle feather, and it was not yet burned and

made brittle by the sun and wind. He had cut the hair too short, and he pulled another from the tail of the near roan and set the snare again. When the reed was curved and strung like a bow, he replaced it carefully in the sand. He laid his forefinger lightly on top of the reed and the reed sprang and the looped end of the hair snapped across his finger and made a white line above the nail. *"Si, bien hecho,"* he said aloud, and without removing the reed from the sand he cocked it again.

The sun rose higher and the old man urged the mares away from the river. Then he was on the old road to San Ysidro. At times he sang and talked to himself above the noise of the wagon: *"Yo heyana oh ... heyana oh ... heyana oh ... Abelito ... tarda mucho en venir. ..."* The mares pulled easily, with their heads low. He held a vague tension on the lines and settled into the ride by force of habit. A lizard ran across the road in front of the mares and crouched on a large flat rock, its tail curved over the edge. Far away a whirlwind moved toward the river, but it soon spun itself out and the air was again perfectly still.

He was alone on the wagon road. The pavement lay on a higher parallel at the base of the hills to the east. The trucks of the town—and those of the lumber camps at Paliza and Vallecitos—made an endless parade on the highway, but the wagon road was used now only by the herdsmen and planters whose fields lay to the south and west. When he came to the place called Seytokwa, Francisco remembered the race for good hunting and harvests. Once he had played a part; he had rubbed himself with soot, and he ran on the wagon road at dawn. He ran so hard that he could feel the sweat fly from his head and arms, though it was winter and the air was filled with snow. He ran until his breath burned in his throat and his feet rose and fell in a strange repetition that seemed apart from all his effort. At last he had overtaken Mariano, who was everywhere supposed to be the best of the long-race runners. For a long way Mariano kept just beyond his reach; then, as they drew near the corrals on the edge of the town,

Francisco picked up the pace. He drew even and saw for an instant Mariano's face, wet and contorted in defeat ... *"Si dió por vencido"* ... and he struck it with the back of his hand, leaving a black smear across the mouth and jaw. And Mariano fell and was exhausted. Francisco held his stride all the way to the Middle, and even then he could have gone on running, for no reason, for only the sake of running on. And that year he killed seven bucks and seven does. Some years afterward, when he was no longer young and his leg had been stiffened by disease, he made a pencil drawing on the first page of a ledger book which he kept with his store of prayer feathers in the rafters of his room. It was the likeness of a straight black man running in the snow. Beneath it was the legend "1889."

He crossed the river below the bridge at San Ysidro. The roan mares strained as they brought the wagon up the embankment and onto the pavement. It was almost noon. The doors of the houses were closed against the heat, and even the usual naked children who sometimes shouted and made fun of him had gone inside. Here and there a dog, content to have found a little shade, raised its head to look but remained outstretched and quiet. Well before he came to the junction, he could hear the slow whine of tires on the Cuba and Bloomfield road. It was a strange sound; it began at a high and descending pitch, passed, and rose again to become at last inaudible, lost in the near clatter of the rig and hoofs—lost even in the slow, directionless motion of the flies. But it was recurrent: another, and another; and he turned into the intersection and drove on to the trading post. He had come about seven miles.

At a few minutes past one, the bus came over a rise far down in the plain and its windows caught for a moment the light of the sun. It grew in the old man's vision until he looked away and limped around in a vague circle and smoothed the front of his new shirt with his hands. "Abelito, Abelito," he repeated under his breath, and he glanced at the wagon and the mares to be sure that everything was in order. He could feel the beat of his heart, and instinctively he drew himself up in the dignity of his age. He heard the sharp wheeze of the brakes as the big bus rolled to a stop in front of the gas pump, and only then did he give attention to it, as if it had taken him by surprise. The door swung open and Abel stepped heavily to the ground and reeled. He was drunk, and he fell against his grandfather and did not know him. His wet lips hung loose and his eyes were half closed and rolling. Francisco's crippled leg nearly gave way. His good straw hat fell off and he braced himself against the weight of his grandson. Tears came to his eyes, and he knew only that he must laugh and turn away from the faces in the windows of the bus. He held Abel upright and led him to the wagon, listening as the bus moved away at last and its tires began to sing upon the road. On the way back to the town, Abel lay ill in the bed of the wagon and Francisco sat bent to the lines. The mares went a little faster on the way home and near the bridge a yellow dog came out to challenge them.

JULY 21

Abel slept through the day and night in his grandfather's house. With the first light of dawn he arose and
went out. He walked swiftly through the dark steets of
the town and all the dogs began to bark. He passed
through the maze of corrals and crossed the highway
and climbed the steep escarpment of the hill. Then he
was high above the town and he could see the whole of
the valley growing light and the far mesas and the
sunlight on the crest of the mountain. In the early
morning the land lay huge and sluggish, discernible
only as a whole, with nothing in relief except its own
sheer, brilliant margin as far away as the eye could see,
and beyond that the nothingness of the sky. Silence lay
like water on the land, and even the frenzy of the dogs
below was feeble and a long time in finding the ear.

"Yañah!" he had yelled when he was five years old,
and he climbed up on the horse behind Vidal and they
went out with their grandfather and the others—some
in wagons, but most on foot and horseback—across the
river to the cacique's field. It was a warm spring morning, and he and Vidal ran ahead of the planters over
the cool, dark furrows of earth and threw stones at the
birds in the gray cottonwoods and elms. Vidal took him
to the face of the red mesa and into a narrow box
canyon which he had never seen before. The bright red
walls were deep, deeper than he could have imagined,
and they seemed to close over him. When they came to
the end, it was dark and cool as a cave. Once he looked
up at the crooked line of the sky and saw that a cloud
was passing and its motion seemed to be that of the
great leaning walls themselves, and he was afraid and

14

cried. When they returned, he went to his grandfather
and watched him dig with the hoe. The work was
nearly finished, and the men broke open the wall of the
ditch, and he stood there watching the foaming brown
water creep among the furrows and go into the broken
earth.

His mother had come in the wagon with Francisco,
and she had made oven bread and rabbit stew and
coffee and round blue cornmeal cakes filled with jam,
coarse and faintly sweet, like figs. They ate on the
ground in groups, according to family and clan, all but
the cacique and governor and the other officials of the
town, who sat at the place of honor nearest the trees.

He did not know who his father was. His father was
a Navajo, they said, or a Sia, or an Isleta, an outsider
anyway, which made him and his mother and Vidal
somehow foreign and strange. Francisco was the man
of the family, but even then he was old and going lame.
And even then the boy could sense his grandfather's
age, just as he knew somehow that his mother was soon
going to die of her illness. It was nothing he was told,
but he knew it anyway and without understanding, as
he knew already the motion of the sun and the seasons.
He was tired then, and he rode home in the wagon
beside his mother and listened to his grandfather sing.
His mother died in October, and for a long time afterward he would not go near her grave, and he remembered that she had been beautiful in a way that he as
well as others could see and her voice had been as soft
as water.

Something frightened him. There was an old woman.
They called her Nicolás *teah-whau* because she had a
white mustache and a hunched back and she would beg
for whiskey on the side of the road. She was a Bahkyush woman, they said, and a witch. She was old
the first time he had seen her, and drunk. She had
screamed at him some unintelligible curse, appearing
out of a cornfield when as a child he had herded the
sheep nearby. And he had run away, hard, until he

came to a clump of mesquite on the bank of an arroyo. There he caught his breath and waited for the snake-killer dog to close the flock and follow. Later, when the sheep had filed into the arroyo and from the bank he could see them all, he dropped a little bread for the snake-killer dog, but the dog had quivered and laid back its ears. Slowly it backed away and crouched, not looking at him, not looking at anything, but listening. Then he heard it, the thing itself. He knew even then that it was only the wind, but it was a stranger sound than any he had ever known. And at the same time he saw the hole in the rock where the wind dipped, struck, and rose. It was larger than a rabbit hole and partly concealed by the chokecherry which grew beside it. The moan of the wind grew loud, and it filled him with dread. For the rest of his life it would be for him the particular sound of anguish.

He was older then, but still a child, and all afternoon he waited outside of the house. The old men went in for the last time, and he heard them pray. He remembered the prayer, and he knew what it meant—not the words, which he had never really heard, but the low sound itself, rising and falling far away in his mind, unmistakable and unbroken. But even then, when he knew what it was that he was waiting for, it seemed a long time before his grandfather called to him. The sun was low, and there was a stillness all around. He went into the room and stood by the side of the bed. His grandfather left him there alone, and he looked at his brother's face. It was terribly thin and colorless, but all the pain was gone from it. Then, under his breath and because he was alone, he spoke his brother's name.

Francisco nudged him awake, and he dressed himself in the bitter cold. He was—how old?—seventeen then, and once he had hunted in clear weather like this and risen as early in order to be near the stream at daybreak. Yes, and the first to come was a mule doe, small and long-haired, unsuspecting but full of latent flight.

He brought the rifle up with no sound that he could hear, but the doe's head sprang up and its body stiffened. Then he stood, and the doe exploded away. The crack of the rifle reverberated among the trees, and he ran to the place where the ground was scarcely marked but for the two small tracks against which the doe had driven itself up and out through the branches. But farther on there was blood, and then the doe itself, lying across the trunk of a dead tree with its tongue out and smoking and the wound full of hot blood, welling out.

Francisco had already hitched the team to the wagon, and they set out. That was January 1, 1937. The moon and stars were out, and as yet there was no sign of the dawn. His face burned with the cold and he huddled over and blew into his hands. And a part of the way he ran beside the horses, swinging his arms high and scaring them to a trot. At Sia they waited in the house of Juliano Medina for the dawn. It was nearly time, and Juliano built a fire and gave them coffee. The deer and antelope had already gone out into the hills, and the crows were dressing in the kiva. When it was gray outside, they went to the Middle and there were already some old people there, Navajos and Domingos in blankets. The singing had begun. Directly the sun shone on the horizon and the deer and the antelope ran down the hills and the crows and the buffalo and the singers came out and the dance began. There was plenty of excitement; a lot of the men had rifles, and they fired them into the air and shouted. He watched the black half-naked crows hopping about and stooping, and he thought of how cold they must be, with the big, gleaming conchos like ice, pressing into their bellies and backs. But it was all right; it was good, that dance, nearly perfect.

Later, when he had drunk some wine, one of Medina's daughters lay down with him outside of the town, on a dune by the river. She was pretty, and laughing all the while—and he, too, though the wine had made him nearly sullen and his laughter was put on and there was

nothing to it. Her body, when at last it shuddered and
went limp, had not been enough for him and he wanted
her again. But she dressed and ran away from him, and
he could not catch her because he was drunk and his
legs would not work for him. He tried to get her back,
but she stood away and laughed at him.

He had seen a strange thing, an eagle overhead with
its talons closed upon a snake. It was an awful, holy
sight, full of magic and meaning.

The Eagle Watchers Society was the sixth to go into
the kiva at the summer and autumn rain retreats. It was
an important society, and it stood apart from the others
in a certain way. This difference—this superiority—had
come about a long time ago. Before the middle of the
last century, there was received into the population of
the town a small group of immigrants from the Tanoan
city of Bahkyula, a distance of seventy or eighty miles
to the east. These immigrants were a wretched people,
for they had experienced great suffering. Their land
bordered upon the Southern Plains, and for many years
they had been an easy mark for marauding bands of
buffalo hunters and thieves. They had endured every
kind of persecution until one day they could stand no
more and their spirit broke. They gave themselves up to
despair and were then at the mercy of the first alien
wind. But it was not a human enemy that overcame
them at last; it was a plague. They were struck down by
so deadly a disease that when the epidemic abated,
there were fewer than twenty survivors in all. And this
remainder, too, should surely have perished among the
ruins of Bahkyula had it not been for these *patrones*,
these distant relatives who took them in at the certain
risk of their own lives and the lives of their children
and grandchildren. It is said that the cacique himself
went out to welcome and escort the visitors in. The
people of the town must have looked narrowly at those
stricken souls who walked slowly toward them, wild in
their eyes with grief and desperation. The Bahkyush
immigrants brought with them little more than the

clothes on their backs, but even in this moment of deep
hurt and humiliation they thought of themselves as a
people. They carried four things that should serve
thereafter to signal who they were: a sacred flute; the
bull and horse masks of Pecos; and the little wooden
statue of their patroness María de los Angeles, whom
they called Porcingula. Now, after the intervening years
and generations, the ancient blood of this forgotten
tribe still ran in the veins of men.

The Eagle Watchers Society was the principal ceremonial organization of the Bahkyush. Its chief, Patiestewa, and all its members were direct descendants of
those old men and women who had made that journey
along the edge of oblivion. There was a look about
these men, even now. It was as if, conscious of having
come so close to extinction, they had got a keener sense
of humility than their benefactors, and paradoxically a
greater sense of pride. Both attributes could be seen in
such a man as old Patiestewa. He was hard, and he
appeared to have seen more of life than had other men.
In their uttermost peril long ago, the Bahkyush had
been fashioned into seers and soothsayers. They had
acquired a tragic sense, which gave to them as a race so
much dignity and bearing. They were medicine men;
they were rainmakers and eagle hunters.

He was not thinking of the eagles. He had been
walking since daybreak down from the mountain where
that year he had broken a horse for the rancher John
Raymond. By the middle of the morning he was on the
rim of the Valle Grande, a great volcanic crater that lay
high up on the western slope of the range. It was the
right eye of the earth, held open to the sun. Of all
places that he knew, this valley alone could reflect the
great spatial majesty of the sky. It was scooped out of
the dark peaks like the well of a great, gathering storm,
deep umber and blue and smoke-colored. The view
across the diameter was magnificent; it was an unbe-
lievably great expanse. As many times as he had been
there in the past, each new sight of it always brought
him up short, and he had to catch his breath. Just

there, it seemed, a strange and brilliant light lay upon the world, and all the objects in the landscape were washed clean and set away in the distance. In the morning sunlight the Valle Grande was dappled with the shadows of clouds and vibrant with rolling winter grass. The clouds were always there, huge, sharply described, and shining in the pure air. But the great feature of the valley was its size. It was almost too great for the eye to hold, strangely beautiful and full of distance. Such vastness makes for illusion, a kind of illusion that comprehends reality, and where it exists there is always wonder and exhilaration. He looked at the facets of a boulder that lay balanced on the edge of the land, and the first thing beyond, the vague misty field out of which it stood, was the floor of the valley itself, pale and blue-green, miles away. He shifted the focus of his gaze, and he could just make out the clusters of dots that were cattle grazing along the river in the faraway plain.

Then he saw the eagles across the distance, two of them, riding low in the depths and rising diagonally toward him. He did not know what they were at first, and he stood watching them, their far, silent flight erratic and wild in the bright morning. They rose and swung across the skyline, veering close at last, and he knelt down behind the rock, dumb with pleasure and excitement, holding on to them with his eyes.

They were golden eagles, a male and a female, in their mating flight. They were cavorting, spinning and spiraling on the cold, clear columns of air, and they were beautiful. They swooped and hovered, leaning on the air, and swung close together, feinting and screaming with delight. The female was full-grown, and the span of her broad wings was greater than any man's height. There was a fine flourish to her motion; she was deceptively, incredibly fast, and her pivots and wheels were wide and full-blown. But her great weight was streamlined and perfectly controlled. She carried a rattlesnake; it hung shining from her feet, limp and curving out in the trail of her flight. Suddenly her wings and tail fanned, catching full on the wind, and for an instant she was still, widespread and spectral in the blue, while her mate flared past and away, turning around in the distance to look for her. Then she began to beat upward at an angle from the rim until she was small in the sky, and she let go of the snake. It fell slowly, writhing and rolling, floating out like a bit of silver thread against the wide backdrop of the land. She held still above, buoyed up on the cold current, her crop and hackles gleaming like copper in the sun. The male swerved and sailed. He was younger than she and a little more than half as large. He was quicker, tighter in his moves. He let the carrion drift by; then suddenly he gathered himself and stooped, sliding down in a blur of motion to the strike. He hit the snake in the head, with not the slightest deflection of his course or speed, cracking its long body like a whip. Then he rolled and swung upward in a great pendulum arc, riding out his momentum. At the top of his glide he let go of the snake in turn, but the female did not go for it. Instead she soared out over the plain, nearly out of sight, like a mote receding into the haze of the far mountain. The male followed, and Abel watched them go, straining to see, saw them veer once, dip and disappear.

Now there was the business of the society. It was getting on toward the end of November, and the eagle hunters were getting ready to set forth to the mountains. He brooded for a time, full of a strange longing; then one day he went to old Patiestewa and told him of what he had seen. "I think you had better let me go," he said. The old chief closed his eyes and thought about it for a long time. Then he answered: "Yes, I had better let you go."

The next day the Bahkyush eagle watchers started out on foot, he among them, northward through the canyon and into the high timber beyond. They were gone for days, holding up here and there at the holy places where they must pray and make their offerings. Early in the morning they came out of the trees on the edge of the Valle Grande. The land fell and reached away in the early light as far as the eye could see, the hills folding together and the gray grass rolling in the plain, and they began the descent. At midmorning they came to the lower meadows in the basin. It was clear and cold, and the air was thin and sharp like a shard of glass. They needed a bait, and they circled out and apart, forming a ring. When the circle was formed, they converged slowly toward the center, clapping and calling out in a high, flat voice that carried only a little way. And as they closed, rabbits began to jump up from the grass and bound. They got away at first, many of them, while the men were still a distance apart, but gradually the ring grew small and the rabbits crept to the center and hid away in the brush. Now and then one of them tried to break away, and the nearest man threw his stick after it. These weapons were small curved clubs, and they were thrown with deadly accuracy by the eagle hunters, so that when the ring was of a certain size and the men only a few feet apart, very few of the animals got away.

He bent close to the gound, his arm cocked and shaking with tension. A great jack-rabbit buck bounded from the grass, straight past him. It struck the ground beyond and sprang again, nearly thirty feet through the air. He spun around and hurled the stick. It struck the jack rabbit a glancing blow just as it bounded again, and the animal slumped in the air and fell heavily to the ground.

The clapping and calling had stopped. He could feel his heart beating and the sweat growing cold on his skin. There was something like remorse or disappointment now that the rabbits were still and strewn about on the ground. He picked one of the dead animals from the brush—it was warm and soft, its eyes shining like porcelain, full of the luster of death—then the great buck, which was not dead but only stunned and frozen with fear. He felt the warm living weight of it in his hands; it was brittle with life, taut with hard, sinewy strength.

When he had bound the bait together and placed it

in the sack, he gathered bunches of tall grass and cut a number of evergreen boughs from the thicket in the plain; these he tied in a bundle and carried in a sling on his back. He went to the river and washed his head in order to purify himself. When all was ready, he waved to the others and started off alone to the cliffs. When he came to the first plateau, he rested and looked out across the valley. The sun was high, and all around there was a pale, dry uniformity of light, a winter glare on the clouds and peaks. He could see a crow circling low in the distance. Higher on the land, where a great slab of white rock protruded from the mountain, he saw the eagle-hunt house; he headed for it. The house was a small tower of stone, built around a pit, hollow and open at the top. Near it was a shrine, a stone shelf in which there was a slight depression. There he placed a prayer offering. He got into the house, and with boughs he made a latticework of beams across the top and covered it with grass. When it was finished, there was a small opening at the center. Through it he raised the rabbits and laid them down on the boughs. He could see here and there through the screen, but his line of vision was vertical, or nearly so, and his quarry would come from the sun. He began to sing, now and then calling out, low in his throat.

The eagles soared southward, high above the Valle Grande. They were almost too high to be seen. From their vantage point the land below reached away on either side to the long, crooked tributaries of the range; down the great open corridor to the south were the wooded slopes and the canyon, the desert and the far end of the earth bending on the sky. They caught sight of the rabbits and were deflected. They veered and banked, lowering themselves into the crater, gathering speed. By the time he knew of their presence, they were low and coming fast on either side of the pit, swooping with blinding speed. The male caught hold of the air and fell off, touching upon the face of the cliff in order to flush the rabbits, while the female hurtled in to take her prey on the run. Nothing happened; the rabbits did not move. She overshot the trap and screamed. She was enraged and she hurled herself around in the air. She swung back with a great clamor of her wings and fell with fury on the bait. He saw her in the instant she struck. Her foot flashed out and one of her talons laid the jack rabbit open the length of its body. It stiffened and jerked, and her other foot took hold of its skull and crushed it. In that split second, when the center of her weight touched down upon the trap, he reached for her. His hands closed upon her legs and he drew her down with all his strength. For one instant only did she recoil, splashing her great wings down upon the beams and boughs—and she very nearly broke from his grasp; but then she was down in the darkness of the well, hooded, and she was still.

At dusk he met with the other hunters in the plain. San Juanito, too, had got an eagle, but it was an aged male and poor by comparison. They gathered around the old eagle and spoke to it, bidding it return with their good will and sorrow to the eagles of the crags. They fixed a prayer plume to its leg and let it go. He watched it back away and stoop, flaring its wings on the ground, glowering, full of fear and suspicion. Then it took leave of the ground and beat upward, clattering through the still shadows of the valley. It gathered speed, driving higher and higher until it reached the shafts of reddish-gold final light that lay like bars across the crater. The light caught it up and set a dark blaze upon it. It leveled off and sailed. Then it was gone from sight, but he looked after it for a time. He could see it still in the mind's eye and hear in his memory the awful whisper of its flight on the wind. It filled him with longing. He felt the great weight of the bird which he held in the sack. The dusk was fading quickly into night, and the others could not see that his eyes were filled with tears.

That night, while the others ate by the fire, he stole away to look at the great bird. He drew the sack open; the bird shivered, he thought, and drew itself up. Bound and helpless, his eagle seemed drab and shapeless in the moonlight, too large and ungainly for flight. The sight of it filled him with shame and disgust. He took hold of its throat in the darkness and cut off its breath.

You ought to do this and that, his grandfather said.

But the old man had not understood, would not understand, only wept, and Abel left him alone. It was time to go, and the old man was away in the fields. There was no one to wish him well or tell him how it would be, and Abel put his hands in his pockets and waited. He had been ready for hours, and he was restless, full of excitement and the dread of going. It was time. He heard the horn and went out and closed the door. And suddenly he had the sense of being all alone, as if he were already miles and months away, gone long ago from the town and the valley and the hills, from everything he knew and had always known. He walked quickly and looked straight ahead, centered upon himself in the onset of loneliness and fear. He had never been in a motorcar before, and he sat by a window in the bus and felt the jar of the engine and the first hard motion of the wheels. The walls of the town fell away. On the climb to the highway the bus leaned and creaked; he felt the lurch and loss of momentum through the succession of gears. There was a lot of speed and sound then, and he tried desperately to take it into account, to know what it meant. Only when it was too late did he remember to look back in the direction of the fields.

This—everything in advance of his going—he could remember whole and in detail. It was the recent past, the intervention of days and years without meaning, of awful calm and collision, time always immediate and confused, that he could not put together in his mind. There was one sharp fragment of recall, recurrent and distinct:

He awoke on the side of a wooded hill. It was afternoon and there were bright, slanting shafts of light on all sides; the ground was covered with damp, matted leaves. He didn't know where he was, and he was alone. No, there were men about, the bodies of men; he could barely see them strewn among the pits, their limbs sprawling away into the litter of leaves, and leaves were falling in the shafts of light, hundreds of leaves, rocking and spiraling down without sound. But there was sound: something low and incessant, almost distant, full of slow, steady motion and approach. It was above and behind him, across the spine of the hill, coming. It moved into the wide wake of silence, taking hold of the silence and swelling huge inside of it, coming. And across the crease of the land there was silence; a thin layer of smoke held still in the distance. The mortar fire had stopped; there someone, some human force far away and out of sight, was making way for the machine that was coming. The silence had awakened him—and the low, even mutter of the machine coming. He didn't know where he was, could not remember having been there and gone to sleep. For hours, days perhaps, the whir and explosion of fire had been the only mooring of his mind to sleep, but now there was nothing but silence and the strange insinuation of the machine upon it. His vision cleared and he saw the countless leaves dip and sail across the splinters of light. The machine concentrated calm, strange and terrific, and it was coming. He rolled over and scanned the ridge, looking into the sun. There was only the dark rim of the hill and the trees edged with light. The sound of the machine brimmed at the ridge, held, and ran over, not intricate now, but whole and deafening. His mouth fell upon the cold, wet leaves, and he began to shake violently. He reached for something, but he had no notion of what it was; his hand closed upon earth and the cold, wet leaves.

Then, through the falling leaves, he saw the machine. It rose up behind the hill, black and massive, looming there in front of the sun. He saw it swell, deepen, and take shape on the skyline, as if it were some upheaval of the earth, the eruption of stone and

eclipse, and all about it the glare, the cold perimeter of
light, throbbing with leaves. For a moment it seemed
apart from the land; its great iron hull lay out against
the timber and the sky, and the center of its weight
hung away from the ridge. Then it came crashing down
to the grade, slow as a waterfall, thunderous, surpassing
impact, *nestling* almost into the splash and boil of
debris. He was shaking violently, and the machine bore
down upon him, came close, and passed him by. A
wind arose and ran along the slope, scattering the
leaves.

And now the silent land bore in upon him as, little
by little, it got hold of the light and shone. The pale
margin of the night receded toward him like a rising
drift, and he waited for it. All the rims of color stood
out upon the hills, and the hills converged at the mouth
of the canyon. That dark cleft might have been a
shadow or a pool of smoke; there was nothing to suggest its distance or its depth, but it held the course of
the river for twenty or thirty miles. The town lay out
for a time on the verge of the day; then the spire of the
mission gleamed and the Angelus rang and the riverside
houses flamed. Still the cold clung to him and the night
was at his back. Just there to the east, the earth was
ashen and the sky on fire. The contour of the black
mesa was clean where the sun ranged like a cloud in
advance of the solstices.

A car appeared on the hills to the north; it crept in
and out of his vision and toward the town and made no
sound until it was directly below him. Then it turned
into the town and wound through the streets and into
the trees at the mission. All the roosters of the town
began to crow and the townspeople stirred and their
thin voices rose up on the air. He could smell the sweet
wine which still kept to his clothing. He had not eaten
in two days, and his mouth tasted of sickness. But the
morning was cold and deep, and he rubbed his hands
together and felt the blood rise and flow.

He stood for a long time, the land still yielding to the

light. He stood without thinking, nor did he move; only
his eyes roved after something ... something. The
white rain-furrowed apron of the hill dropped under
him thirty feet to the highway. The last patches of
shade vanished from the river bottom and the chill
grew dull on the air. He picked his way downward, and
the earth and stones rolled at his feet. He felt the
tension at his knees, and then the weight of the sun on
his head and hands. The dry light of the valley rose up,
and the land became hard and pale.

The day had begun as usual at the mission. It was a
feast of martyrs, and Father Olguin took down the
scarlet chasuble from its place in the wardrobe. He was
a small, swarthy man with sharp features, and his hair
had gone prematurely gray in part. He was not an old
man, but his shoulders sagged and he moved about
rather slowly as the result of an illness which he had
suffered years ago in his native Mexico, so that from a
distance he appeared to be aged and worn out. One of
his eyes was clouded over with a blue, transparent film,
and the lid drooped almost closed. Had it not been for
that, he would have been thought of as good-looking in
the face. He had crushed out a cigarette before coming
into the sacristy; his fingers were stained with tobacco.
    It was cold and dark in the sacristy. The old man
Francisco had already knelt at the small glass panel
which opened upon the chapel altar, and a small, sleepy
boy whose name was Bonifacío stood in the corner,
putting on a faded red cassock. There was a shuffle and
coughing of people in the pews beyond the wall. It was
already a minute past the half hour. *"Ándale, hombre!"* the old man whispered sharply, and the boy
started and hurried out to light the candles, half unbut-
toned. The old man watched him through the glass. He
loved the candles; loved to see how the flame came
upon the wicks, how slow it was to take hold and flare
up.
    Father Olguin heard the car come over the boards at
the irrigation ditch and stop, and he went to the win-

dow and looked out. There were smoky lines of sunlight through the trees; they fell in soft, bright patterns on the yard, and the wire fence which ran along the street was overgrown with blue and violet morning-glories. A pale, dark-haired young woman in a gray raincoat got out of the car and stood for a moment looking around. Then she placed a blue scarf about her head, opened the gate, and walked through the yard to the chapel. He followed her with his good eye all the way to the door, trying to imagine who she was; he had never seen her before. Her footsteps sounded in the aisle, and he turned and took up the chalice and followed Bonifacío out to the altar.

The woman did not receive the sacrament of communion, and it was not until afterward, when she came to the door of the rectory, that he saw her face to face. She was older than he had supposed, and she did not seem quite so pale as before.

"How do you do?" she said. "I am Mrs. Martin St. John," and she offered her hand to him.

"How do you do? You have not been here before."

"No, I'm a visitor. I am staying in the canyon for a time, at Los Ojos."

"Will you come in?"

He showed her through the hall and into a small reception room which contained a round black table and several chairs. He offered her a cigarette, which she declined, and they sat down.

"Please forgive me for calling on you so early in the day, Father—I realize that you probably have your breakfast now—but I should like to ask your help in a small matter that has just come up. And of course I wanted to meet you and assist at Mass."

"Of course, I'm glad you came. I saw you drive up, you know, and I wondered who you were."

"We live in California, my husband and I, Los Angeles. . . . This is beautiful country; I have never been here before."

"No? In that case, welcome. *Bienvenido a la tierra del encanto.*"

"The sky is so blue. It was like water, very still and deep, when I drove through the canyon a while ago."

"Your husband, he is with you?"

"No—no. He had to stay in California. He is a doctor, you see; it's very hard for him to get away."

"Of course. Well, I know some of the people at Los Ojos. Do you have relatives there by any chance?"

"No. Actually, Martin wanted me to try the mineral baths. I have had a soreness in my back for several weeks."

"They say that the spring water is very healthful."

"Yes," she said.

For a moment she seemed lost in thought. The sun had cleared the trees, and it shone directly into the room; the tabletop was a disc of bright purplish light, and there were innumerable particles of dust floating visibly in the air. Bees swarmed at the window and wagons passed in the street. The horses blew and shook to settle the traces about them, pulling for the river and the fields. A soft breeze stirred in the room; it was fresh and cool and delicious.

The priest regarded his guest discreetly, wondering that her physical presence should suddenly dawn upon him so. She was more nearly beautiful than he had thought at first. Her hair was long and very dark, so that ordinarily it appeared to be black; but in a certain light, as now, it acquired a dark auburn sheen. She was too thin, he thought, and her nose was a trifle long. But her skin was clear and lovely, and her eyes and mouth were made up carefully and well. She had leaned back in the chair and crossed her legs, which were slim and bare and expressive. In this light she seemed pale to him again, and her hair threaded with the finest running lines of light, silver and bronze. Her hands were small and smooth and white; there was a pale pink lacquer on her nails.

"You said something about needing help?"

"Oh, yes. I wonder if you know of anyone here who will do some work for me. I have bought some wood that has to be cut. You see, I have taken a house at Los

Ojos—the large white house below the forestry station—"

"The Benevides house?"

"Yes, that's it. Well, there is only the wood stove in the kitchen, and I need to have some wood cut for it."

"How much wood is there?"

"Quite a lot, I think—I'm sorry; I don't know how to measure it. One of the men in the village brought it yesterday, but he works in the mountains and hasn't time to cut it up. I shall be happy to pay whatever . . . I thought that perhaps one of the Indians—"

"Certainly. There are some boys here. . . . I can ask the sacristan."

In the noon and early afternoon there was no sign of life in the town. The streets were empty and sterile in the white glare of the sun. There were no shadows, no dimensions of depth to the walls; even the doorways and windows were flat and impenetrable. There was no motion on the air, and the white dust burned in the streets. At this hour of the day, especially, the town seemed to disappear into the earth. Everything in the valley inclined to the color of dust.

Earlier Abel had returned to his grandfather's house, but the old man was not there. Nothing had yet passed between them, no word, no sign of recognition. He had been hungry, but his mouth was sour and dry; he could think of nothing that he wanted to eat, and his hunger grew dull and passed away. His mind turned on him again in the silence and the heat, and he could not hold still. He paced about in the rooms; the rooms were small and bare, and the walls were bare and clean and white. In the late afternoon he went to the river and walked along the river to the crossing. He made his way along the incline at the edge of the cultivated fields to the long row of foothills at the base of the red mesa. When the first breeze of the evening rose up in the shadow that fell across the hills, he sat down and looked out over the green and yellow blocks of farmland. He could see his grandfather, others, working below in the sunlit fields. The breeze was very faint, and it bore a scent of earth and grain; and for a moment everything was all right with him. He was at home.

JULY 24

Abel came to the Benevides house on Tuesday. He would cut the wood for three dollars. Angela St. John had been prepared to bargain, but there was no indulgence in him, no concession to trade; he had simply, once and for all, shut her off. It remained for her to bring about a vengeance. She smiled and looked down from an upstairs window as he chopped the wood.

She had never seen a man put his back to his work before. Always there had been a kind of resistance, an angle of motion or of will. But it was different with him; he gave himself up to it. He took up the axe easily, and his strokes were clean and deep. The bit fell into the flesh of the wood and the flesh curled and spun away. He worked rocking on his hips, his feet set wide apart and his neck bowed and swollen out. She watched, full of wonder, taking his motion apart. He raised the axe, drawing the curve of the handle out and across his waist, sliding back his hand until it lay against the black metal wedge; then his shoulders turned and wound up the spine. There was an instant in which the coil of his body was set and all his strength was poised in the breach of time, then the infinite letting go. He leaned into the swing and drove; the blade flashed and struck, and the wood gaped open. Angela caught her breath and said, "I see." A soft breeze blew in at the window and touched her hair at the temples. The sunlight struck silver on the leaves of the fruit trees, and she grew restless and intent.

Now, now that she could see, she was aware of some useless agony that was spent upon the wood, some hurt she could not have imagined until now. And later, when she looked away, she half listened to him still.

Beyond the close, damp fragrance of rose leaves and tea, there was nothing but his labor in the day. She would have her bath and read from the lives of saints. Perhaps she would put down her head and close her eyes. That she could do to the makeshift music of the day and night, and even now there was a sound of bees, of dark water lapping—and the ring of the axe against the wood, steady, unceasing.

Angela paced in the downstairs. Always, when she was left alone at a certain hour in the afternoon, she was a shade beside herself. In the lowest brilliance of the day she wondered who she was. At such times now, when a strange blush and dizziness came upon her, she imagined the child within her, placed her hands low upon her body and drew the child up close to her heart, spoke to it in a voice that wavered like a flame. "My darling," she would say. "Oh, my darling!" and she looked for some sign of disaster on the wind. Now and then she watched the birds that hied and skittered in the sky, but the birds always went away, and then the sky was empty again and eternal beyond all hope.

The axe rang out against her, the incessant sound, hollow, dying away at the source. Once she had seen an animal slap at the water, a badger or a bear. She would have liked to touch the soft muzzle of a bear, the thin black lips, the great flat head. She would have liked to cup her hand to the wet black snout, to hold for a moment the hot blowing of the bear's life. She went out of the house and sat down on the stone steps of the porch. He was there rearing above the wood. The canyon was cut out of shadows. The final sunlight had risen to the rim of the canyon wall above the orchard, and there it flamed on the face of the rock. A hummingbird hung among the hollyhocks, and dusk lay in upon the orchard, smudging the leaves. Her feet were naked in mules, and her arms and legs were bare. There was a chill rising up in the canyon, but she was not alive to it; there was a vague heat upon her. He placed the axe deep in the block and came to her.

She sucked at her cheeks and let the initiative lie, to see what he would do.

"There is gum in it," he said at last. "It will burn for a long time."

He looked at her without the trace of a smile, but his voice was soft and genial, steady. He would give her no clear way to be contemptuous of him. She considered.

"Shall I pay you now?" she asked.

He thought about it, but it was clear that he did not care one way or another.

"I'll cut the rest of it Friday or Saturday. You can pay me then."

It offended her that he would not buy and sell. Still, she knew how to learn at her own expense, and eventually she would make good the least investment of her pride. It was just now, for the time being, that she must hold her ground and wait. There was a silence between them. He continued to stand off in the failing light, his still, black eyes just wide of her own. He did not move a muscle.

"You have done a day's work," she said, wondering why she had said it, and he stood there. There was no reply, nothing.

"Well, then," she said, "you will come on Friday? Or did you say Saturday?"

But he made no answer. She was full of irritation. She knew only how to persist, but she had already begun to sense that it was of no use; and that made her seethe.

"You will have to make up your mind, you see, or else I may not be here when you come."

His face darkened, but he hung on, dumb and immutable. He would not allow himself to be provoked. It was easy, natural for him to stand aside, hang on. He seemed to be watching from far away something that was happening within her, private, commonplace, nothing in itself. His reserve was too much for her. She would have liked to throw him off balance, to startle and appall him, to make an obscene gesture, perhaps, or to say, "How would you like a white woman? My white belly and my breasts, my painted fingers and my feet?" But it would have been of no use. She was certain that he would not even have been ashamed for her—or in the least surprised.

And yet, in some curious way, he was powerless, too. She could see that now. There he stood, dumb and docile at her pleasure, not knowing, she supposed, how even to take his leave. In the dark she could no longer see him. She heard him walk away.

She thought of her body and could not understand that it was beautiful. She could think of nothing more vile and obscene than the raw flesh and blood of her body, the raveled veins and the gore upon her bones. And now the monstrous fetal form, the blue, blind, great-headed thing growing within and feeding upon her. From the time she was a child and first saw her own blood, how it brimmed in a cut on the back of her hand, she had conceived a fear and disgust of her body which nothing could make her forget. She did not fear death, only the body's implication in it. And at odd moments she wished with all her heart to die by fire, fire of such intense heat that her body should dissolve in it all at once. There must be no popping of fat or any burning on of the bones. Above all she must give off no stench of death.

She went out into the soft yellow light that fell from the windows and that lay upon the ground and the pile of wood. She knelt down and picked up the cold, hard lengths of wood and laid them in the crook of her arm. They were sharp and seamed at the ends where the axe had shaped them like pencil points, and they smelled of resin. When again she stood, she inadvertently touched the handle of the axe; it was stiff and immovable in the block, and cold. She felt with the soles of her feet the chips of wood which lay all about on the ground, among the dark stones and weeds. The long black rim of the canyon wall lay sheer on the dark, silent sky. She stood, remembering the sacramental violence which had touched the wood. One of the low plateaus, now invisible above her, had been gutted long ago by fire, and in the day she had seen how the black spines of the dead trees stood out. She imagined the fire which had run upon them, burning out their sweet amber gum. Then they were flayed by the fire and their deep fibrous flesh cracked open, and among the cracks the wood was burned into charcoal and ash, and in the sun each facet of the dead wood shone low like velvet and felt like velvet to the touch, and left the soft death of itself on the hands that touched it.

She took the wood inside and laid it down on a fireplace grate. It caught fire so slowly that she did not see it happen, though she looked hard for it. Then she watched the yellow-white flames curl around the wood, seeming never to lay hold of the hard, vital core.

Later that evening Father Olguin came to the Benevides house.

"Tomorrow is the feast of Santiago," he said. "There is a celebration in the town. Will you come?"

"All right. Thank you."

He wanted to stay, to look at her and listen to her voice, but she was brooding, absent, and he said good night.

Angela thought of Abel, of the way he looked at her—like a wooden Indian—his face cold and expressionless. A few days before she had seen the corn dance at Cochiti. It was beautiful and strange. It had seemed to her that the dancers meant to dance forever in that slow, deliberate way. There was something so grave and mysterious in it, those old men chanting in the sun, and the dancers so . . . so terribly *serious* in what they were doing. No one of them ever smiled. Somehow that seemed important to her just now. The dancers had looked straight ahead, to the exclusion of everything, but she had not thought about that at the time. And they had not smiled. They were grave, so unspeakably grave. They were not merely sad or formal or devout; it was nothing like that. It was simply that they were grave, distant, intent upon something that she could not see. Their eyes were held upon some vision out of range, something away in the end of distance, some reality that she did not know, or even suspect. What was it that they saw? Probably they saw nothing after all, nothing at all. But then that was the trick, wasn't it? To see nothing at all, nothing in the absolute. To see beyond the landscape, beyond every shape and shadow and color, *that* was to see nothing. That was to be free and finished, complete, spiritual. To see nothing slowly and by degrees, at last; to see first the pure, bright colors of near things, then all pollutions of color, all things blended and vague and dim in the distance, to see finally beyond the clouds and the pale wash of the sky—the none and nothing beyond that. To say "beyond the mountain," and to mean it, to mean, simply, beyond everything for which the mountain stands, of which it signifies the being. Somewhere, if only she could see it, there was neither nothing nor anything. And there, just there, *that* was the last reality. Even so, in the same attitude of non-being, Abel had cut the wood. She had not seen into his eyes until it was too late, until they had returned upon everything. And then they were soft, full of color, ranging; they had seen into her, through her, even, but his vision had fallen short of the reality that mattered last and most. He, too, had come upon her everyday dense, impenetrable world. For that reason and no other she could stand up to him. She set her mind at ease and looked into the fire. It had gone to embers, and there were only the intermittent blue and yellow flames, small and going out.

JULY 25

This, according to Father Olguin:

Santiago rode southward into Mexico. Although his horse was sleek and well bred, he himself was dressed in the guise of a peon. When he had journeyed a long way, he stopped to rest at the house of an old man and his wife. They were poor and miserable people, but they were kind and gracious, too, and they bade Santiago welcome. They gave him cold water to slake his thirst and cheerful words to comfort him. There was nothing in the house to eat; but a single, aged rooster strutted back and forth in the yard. The rooster was their only possession of value, but the old man and woman killed and cooked it for their guest. That night they gave him their bed while they slept on the cold ground. When morning came, Santiago told them who he was. He gave them his blessing and continued on his way.

He rode on for many days, and at last came to the royal city. That day the king proclaimed that there should be a great celebration and many games, dangerous contests of skill and strength. Santiago entered the games. He was derided at first, for everyone supposed him to be a peon and a fool. But he was victorious, and as a prize he was allowed to choose and marry one of the king's daughters. He chose a girl with almond-shaped eyes and long black hair, and he made ready to return with her to the north. The king was filled with resentment to think that a peon should carry his daughter away, and he conceived a plan to kill the saint. Publicly he ordered a company of soldiers to escort the travelers safely on their journey home. But under cover he directed that Santiago should be put to death as soon as the train was away from the city gates.

Now by a miracle Santiago brought forth from his mouth the rooster, whole and alive, which the old man and woman had given him to eat. The rooster warned him at once of what the soldiers meant to do and gave him the

spur from its right leg. When the soldiers turned upon him,
Santiago slew them with a magic sword.

At the end of the journey Santiago had no longer any
need of his horse, and the horse spoke to him and said:
"Now you must sacrifice me for the good of the people."
Accordingly, Santiago stabbed the horse to death, and
from its blood there issued a great herd of horses, enough
for all the Pueblo people. After that, the rooster spoke to
Santiago and said: "Now you must sacrifice me for the
good of the people." And accordingly Santiago tore the
bird apart with his bare hands and scattered the remains
all about on the ground. The blood and feathers of the
bird became cultivated plants and domestic animals, enough
for all the Pueblo people.

The late afternoon of the feast of Santiago was still
and hot, and there were no clouds in the sky. The river
was low, and the grape leaves had begun to curl in the
fire of the sun. The pale yellow grass on the river plain
was tall, for the cattle and sheep had been taken to
graze in the high meadows, and alkali lay like frost in
the cracked beds of the irrigation ditches. It was a pale
midsummer day, two or three hours before sundown.

Father Olguin went with Angela St. John out of the
rectory. They walked slowly, talking together, along the
street which ran uphill toward the Middle. There were
houses along the north side of the street, patches of
grapes and corn and melons on the south. There had
been no rain in the valley for a long time, and the dust
was deep in the street. By one of the houses a thin old
man tended his long hair, careless of their passing. He
was bent forward, and his hair reached nearly to the
ground. His head was cocked, so that the hair hung all
together on one side of his face and in front of the
shoulder. He brushed slowly the inside of it, downward
from the ear, with a bunch of quills. His hands worked
easily, intimately, with the coarse, shining hair, in
which there was no appearance of softness, except that
light moved upon it as on a pouring of oil.

They saw faces in the dark windows and doorways
of the houses, half in hiding, watching with wide, sol-

emn eyes. The priest paused among them, and Angela
drew away from him a little. She was among the houses
of the town, and there was an excitement all around, a
ceaseless murmur under the sound of the drum, lost in
back of the walls, apart from the dead silent light of the
afternoon. When she had got too far ahead, she waited
beside a windmill and a trough, around which there
was a muddy black ring filled with the tracks of animals. In the end of July the town smelled of animals,
and smoke, and sawed lumber, and the sweet, moist
smell of bread that has been cut open and left to stand.

When they came to the Middle, there was a lot of
sound going on. The people of the town had begun to
gather along the walls of the houses, and a group of
small boys ran about, tumbling on the ground and
shouting. The Middle was an ancient place, nearly a
hundred yards long by forty wide. The smooth, packed
earth was not level, as it appeared at first to be, but
rolling and concave, rising slightly to the walls around
it so that there were no edges or angles in the dry clay
of the ground and the houses; there were only the soft
contours and depressions of things worn down and
away in time. From within, the space appeared to be
enclosed, but there were narrow passages at the four
corners and a wide opening midway along the south
side, where once there had been a house; there was now
a low, uneven ruin of earthen bricks, nearly indistin-
guishable from the floor and the back wall of the
recess. There Angela and the priest entered and turned,
waiting, conscious of themselves, to be absorbed in the
sound and motion of the town.

The oldest houses, those at the west end and on the
north side, were tiered, two and three stories high, and
clusters of men and women stood about on the roofs.
The drummer was there, on a rooftop, still beating on
the drum, slowly, exactly in time, with only a quick,
nearly imperceptible motion of the hand, standing perfectly still and even-eyed, old and imperturbable. Just
there, in sight of him, the deep vibration of the drum
seemed to Angela scarcely louder, deeper, than it had

an hour before and a half mile away, when she was in a
room of the rectory, momentarily alone with it and
borne upon it. And it should not have seemed less had
she been beyond the river and among the hills; the
drum held sway in the valley, like the breaking of
thunder far away, echoing on and on in a region out of
time. One has only to take it for granted, she thought,
like a storm coming up, and the certain, rare downfall
of rain. She pulled away from it and caught sight of
window frames, blue and white, earthen ovens like the
hives of bees, vigas, dogs and flies. Equidistant from all
the walls of the Middle there was a fresh hole in the
ground, about eight inches in diameter, and a small
mound of sandy earth.

In a little while the riders came into the west end in
groups of three and four, on their best animals. There
were seven or eight men and as many boys. They
crossed the width of the Middle and doubled back in
single file along the wall. Abel rode one of his grandfather's roan black-maned mares and sat too rigid in the
saddle, too careful of the gentle mare. For the first time
since coming home he had done away with his uni-
form. He had put on his old clothes: Levi's and a wide
black belt, a gray work shirt, and a straw hat with a
low crown and a wide, rolled brim. His sleeves were
rolled high, and his arms and hands were newly sunburned. The appearance of one of the men was striking. He was large, lithe, and white-skinned; he wore
little round colored glasses and rode a fine black horse
of good blood. The black horse was high-spirited, and
the white man held its head high on the reins and kept
the stirrups free of it. He was the last in line, and when
he had taken his place with the others in the shade of
the wall, an official of the town brought a large white
rooster from one of the houses. He placed it in the hole
and moved the dirt in upon it until it was buried to the
neck. Its white head jerked from side to side, so that its
comb and wattles shook and its hackles were spread
out on the sand. The townspeople laughed to see it so,
buried and fearful, its round, unblinking eyes yellow

and bright in the dying day. The official moved away,
and the first horse and rider bolted from the shade.
Then, one at a time, the others rode down upon the
rooster and reached for it, holding to the horns of their
saddles and leaning sharply down against the shoulders
of the mounts. Most of the animals were untrained,
and they drew up when their riders leaned. One and
then another of the boys fell to the ground, and the
townspeople jeered in delight. When it came Abel's
turn, he made a poor showing, full of caution and
gesture. Angela despised him a little; she would remember that, but for the moment her attention was spread
over the whole fantastic scene, and she felt herself
going limp. With the rush of the first horse and rider all
her senses were struck at once. The sun, low and
growing orange, burned on her face and arms. She
closed her eyes, but it was there still, the brilliant
disorder of motion: the dark and darker gold of the
earth and earthen walls and the deep incisions of shade
and the vague, violent procession of centaurs. So unintelligible the sharp sound of voices and hoofs, the odor
of animals and sweat, so empty of meaning it all was,
and yet so full of appearance. When he passed in front
of her at a walk, on his way back, she was ready again
to deceive. She smiled at him and looked away.

The white man was large and thickset, powerful and
deliberate in his movements. The black horse started
fast and ran easily, even as the white man leaned down
from it. He got hold of the rooster and took it from the
ground. Then he was upright in the saddle, suddenly,
without once having shifted the center of his weight
from the spine of the running horse. He reined in hard,
so that the animal tucked in its haunches and its hoofs
plowed in the ground. Angela thrilled to see it handled
so, as if the white man were its will and all its shivering
force were drawn to his bow. A perfect commotion, full
of symmetry and sound. And yet there was something
out of place, some flaw in proportion or design, some
unnatural thing. She keened to it, whatever it was, and
an old fascination returned upon her. The black horse

whirled. The white man looked down the Middle toward the other riders and held the rooster up and away in his left hand while its great wings beat the air. He started back on the dancing horse, slowly, along the south wall, and the townspeople gave him room. Then he faced her, and Angela saw that under his hat the pale yellow hair was thin and cut close to the scalp; the tight skin of the head was visible and pale and pink. The face was huge and mottled white and pink, and the thick, open lips were blue and violet. The flesh of the jowls was loose, and it rode on the bone of the jaws. There were no brows, and the small, round black glasses lay like pennies close together and flat against the enormous face. The albino was directly above her for one instant, huge and hideous at the extremity of the terrified bird. It was then her eyes were drawn to the heavy, bloodless hand at the throat of the bird. It was like marble or chert, equal in the composure of stone to the awful frenzy of the bird, and the bright red wattles of the bird lay still among the long blue nails, and the comb on the swollen heel of the hand. And then he was past. He rode in among the riders, and they, too, parted for him, watching to see whom he would choose, respectful, wary, and on edge. After a long time of playing the game, he rode beside Abel, turned suddenly upon him, and began to flail him with the rooster. Their horses wheeled, and the others drew off. Again and again the white man struck him, heavily, brutally, upon the chest and shoulders and head, and Abel threw up his hands, but the great bird fell upon them and beat them down. Abel was not used to the game, and the white man was too strong and quick for him. The roan mare lunged, but it was hemmed in against the wall; the black horse lay close against it, keeping it off balance, coiled and wild in its eyes. The white man leaned and struck, back and forth, with only the mute malice of the act itself, careless, undetermined, almost composed in some final, preeminent sense. Then the bird was dead, and still he swung it down and across, and the neck of the bird was broken and the flesh torn

open and the blood splashed everywhere about. The
mare hopped and squatted and reared, and Abel hung
on. The black horse stood its ground, cutting off every
line of retreat, pressing upon the terrified mare. It was
all a dream, a tumultuous shadow, and before it the
fading red glare of the sun shone on bits of silver and
panes of glass and softer on the glowing, absorbent
walls of the town. The feathers and flesh and entrails of
the bird were scattered about on the ground, and the
dogs crept near and crouched, and it was finished. Here
and there the townswomen threw water to finish it in
sacrifice.

It is somehow in keeping, she thought afterward, this
strange exhaustion of her whole being. She was bone
weary, and her feet slipped down in the sand of the
street, and it was nearly beyond her to walk. Like this,
her body had been left to recover without her when
once and for the first time, having wept, she had lain
with a man; and it had been the same sacrificial hour of
the day. She had been too tired for guilt and gladness,
and she lay for a long time on the edge of sleep, empty
of the least desire, in the warm current of her blood.
Like this, though she could not then have known—the
sheer black land above the orchards and the walls, the
scarlet sky and the three-quarter moon.

Afterward, when Angéla had gone back to the Benevides house, Father Olguin went upstairs to his room
and said his office. A few minutes past eleven he came
down again and made a fire in the kitchen stove and
warmed a pot of coffee. He was tired, but as usual he
could not sleep until it was morning. He required only
a little sleep, and he always awoke with a strange sense
of urgency. It was late at night that he liked best to use
his mind, to read and write with cigarettes and black
coffee. Then, alone with himself, he could take stock of
all his resources and prospects, and he could find his
place among them. He had removed his soutane and put
on a worn pair of canvas trousers and a sweat shirt that
hung nearly to his knuckles and knees. It had grown

cold in the downstairs, and he closed the kitchen door
and sat down at the table. He had brought from his
room a book which he had found not long after his
arrival in the town among the parish records. The
coffee and the heat of the fire warmed him. There was
no sound in the house, save the seldom crackling of the
fire, and he could hear outside the drone of the genera-
tor, not quite steady, and the yellow ceiling light of the
kitchen swelled and failed to its pitch. For several
minutes he savored the coffee and smoke and regarded
the closed book absently, waiting for the long day to
end inside of him. He stroked the stubble of beard at his
throat and at last set the empty cup aside and crushed
the cigarette out and lit another. A cockroach ran from
the floor of the pantry in the corner of the room and
stood sud⁴enly very still for a moment where a part of
the gray linoleum had been worn away and the wood of
the floor was bare and brown. Then it was gone.

The book was a kind of journal, old and bound in
leather. The boards were visible and frayed at the
corners, and here and there the leather was cracked and
had begun to peel. He opened it with the tips of his
fingers and moved the tips of his fingers slowly upon
the dim lines of script, as if it were somehow possible to
feel the raised shape of the words. The leaves were
yellow and brittle at the margins, and dimly ruled in
brown. And the script where he began to read was
brown and even and precise, nearly the hand of a scriv-
ener. Under the year 1874:

16th November

This morning a new wind & snow. Again I am consumed
in coughing & can scarcely say Thy Mass. Lord Thy ser-
vant & mine Viviano said again María bear-HEE-nay et OMO
FATUOUS! Be Thou pleased to forgive Thy black & bleating
lamb. His little brother Francisco did not come it was so
cold tho' Thou knowest how well he loves to swing on the
bell rope & walk on the hem of his cassock. With Thine
Almighty help not otherways he will be ready next month
to sing Thee the Glory of Thy Birth. There is so little

time after all & Thou hast said to me Nicolás thy whole
life thou art the midwife of My Coming. Yes & I await
Thee still.

17th November

But if one among thee asks his father for a loaf will he
hand him a stone? Or for a fish will he for a fish hand him
a serpent? Or if he asks for an egg will he hand him a
scorpion?

19th November

Didst Thou see? Today when Thou wert broken on my
tongue didst Thou see me shake? I have never loved Thee
more & I shall never love Thee less again. No not less
tho' I be hale in the hour & whole. I dare not pray for it!

But this afternoon the sun did shine thro' the storm &
I took heart in it or so until I went in to see old Tomacita
Fragua. She declined in the bad weather near to death & I
am glad to have gone there at once & do commend her
wretched soul to Thee. Coming back I was taken off in
another fit & leant over & spat blood on the snow & was
it Thine?

I see now it will be clear tomorrow.

22d November

Watch ye therefore for ye know neither the day nor the
hour. Tomacita Fragua died this late morning & again I
was not called to it. But the son-in-law Diego came in the
afternoon & gave me leave to make the burial. I saw they
had finished with her according to their dark custom &
there was blue & yellow meal about on the floor. This
rubbed on the stone fine as pollen almost & 4 feathers in
the dead hands turkey & brown eagle. They had wound
her in a blanket tight & I saw as not before her belly was
swoln as with child & already an awful stench. I marveled
it was so soon. We made a little procession to the Campo
Santo: Antonio & Carlos with her on the ladder & Viviano
to assist me. Juan Chinana my good Sacristan too tho' he
was there already with the War Captain & had made the
grave on the southeast by the arroyo & had already a little
whitewashed cross of willow & thread. Then he Juan

shoveled earth on her but it was frozen under the sand &
hard to break the big pieces & some I thought would have
given her hurt if she had been alive.

Evening. Am I not yet constrained into Thee? When I
cannot speak Thy Name I want Thee most to restore me.
Restore me! Thy Spirit comes upon me & I am too frail
for Thee!

5 hrs since I have writ here & now I witness here that I
am awakened coughing by something of the cold & dark
terrible & strange & I fell out on my knees & rattled with
cold on the floor. It seemed as tho' I had done some evil
& I

12th December

Did the little boys not serve Thee & Thy Mother well?
I gave Viviano 1 sweet & Francisco 2.

25th December

Lord Thy Nativity. For this Day in the town of David a
Saviour has been born unto Thee Who is Christ the Lord.

Thou sayest Nicolás take up thy strength in Me for the
day shall come that I must take thy heft upon My back &
go out into the streets. Yes Lord yes yes yes. I fed upon
Thee in the Night & still I am full of Thee & have taken
no thing other nor shall I this Day & Night

A 3d or half attendance Thy 1st Mass & some good
Spanish & Sias too tho' many more afterward. I must think
Don De Lay O has not finished Thee or Thou art too late
on the way. But his little cedar of Thy Mother is truly a
wonderful & holy likeness & favors even His Excellency's
Conquistadora tho' it is not so big & has not real hair. So
Thou wert again this year our Blessed Infant of Prague &
Thy Crown suitable I think tho' it lay in the straw & Thy
visitors were Thine own brute creatures. Ynocencía Thine
Herald Angel again. San Juanito Thy Father Joseph. Ave-
lino again & Pasqual & Viviano Thy Wise Men. Lupita
Thine ass & wiser. Augustín & Francisco Thy lambs who
have still the bigness of lambs & the sense. But they
sang & I think Thou must have heard no matter Thou hadst
been deaf even & I pray fervently Thou were not sleeping!

I have given Thee over in procession to Domingo
Gachupin his house until Epiphany. Mind well Thy Patrons

Little One for I am excluded from Thee. Now the chanting
& the drums & I have no part of it & I am by myself & tired.
I hope Francisco will come in for a little while in the
morning.

Under the year 1875:

5th January

Thy Circumcision. When 8 days were fulfilled for the
Circumcision of the Child His Name was called Jesus the
Name given Him by the Angel before He was Conceived in
the Womb.

Yesterday late I returned from Cuba & near was thrown
down on the way where a rabbit jumped up & I was
gone almost to sleep in the cold. So with Tío & he reared
& ran & today is worse lame tho' I did walk with him the
remainder. Avenicío Lucero & Jesús Baca did die at Cuba
since I was the last time there. María Delgado confesses 9
mortal & 32 venial sins! & wonders exceedingly at the 9
as if they had been miracles.

I heard today of a strange thing here on the 3d & so
went to see a child born to Manuelita & Diego Fragua. It
is what is called an albino whiter than any child I have
seen before tho' it had been of the white race. It is dead
& raw about its eyes & mouth tho' otherways hale I think
& there is a meager white hair on its head like an old man
& its crying is very little to hear. I advise to baptize this
same day & do so at 3 o'clock. It is given a name Juan
Reyes.

Night. As now every night a chill comes on me & I burn
against it as I can sleep. I am better in the day but 4 or
5 fits at least & of some duration. I begin now to think
much upon my going out in the weather yet Thou hast
given me a considerable work. I have no taste but for
Thee & take only a little bread & meal in water tho' Francisco gave me a fine piece of venison which before I liked
above mutton or beef.

There followed numerous pages in which the entries
were composed almost entirely of texts and homilies.
Father Olguin passed these by and opened the book to
a later place. There was a letter inserted which Fray

Nicolás had written to an unnamed person, perhaps a relative. Although he had read the letter and most of the journal once or twice before, Father Olguin saw for the first time that the hand was now changed in certain minute details. Something of its former control was lost, some quality of patience or intent. He took up the letter carefully in his hands and unfolded it. He felt curiously busy with it, as if it were his own creation and he were setting it down as a testament to his faith, to be written and read again at a later time.

17th. October. 1888

My dearest brother J. M.,
  You have my best thanks for the books & paper & God in His infinite Goodness will reward you according to your generosity. Be assured my brother that I am as well as can be expected. The wonder of it. I see in my diary it is 10 years & more since you came to me on my deathbed & gave me your richest blessing. Truly I am Lazarus & you the witness of it. You may say with me as it is writ Cor. I. O death where is thy victory? O death where is thy sting? But all this time I have not regained my whole strength & that most sinister Angel is not once out of my sight. I watch for him to come near me but he mocks & tarries. He tarries brother. I am put aside for him I know it. I must suppose you think me fanciful. Listen brother I heard him speak your name. You are pleased to tell me how you prosper but your time will come. Be wise to say goodbye every day to your wife Catherine for her time will come & your children their time will come.
  Listen I told you of Francisco & was right to say it. He is evil & desires to do me some injury & this after I befriended him all his life. Preserve this I write to you that you may make him responsible if I die. He is one of them & goes often in the kiva & puts on their horns & hides & does worship that Serpent which even is the One our most ancient enemy. Yet he is unashamed to make one of my sacristans & brother I am most fearful to forbid it. You will be reviled I believe to hear that he lays hold of the paten & the Host & so defiles me in the sight of my enemies. Where is the Most Holy Spirit that he is not struck

down at that moment? I have some expectation of it always & am disappointed. Why am I betrayed who cannot desire to betray? I am not deceived that he has been with Porcingula Pecos a vile one I assure you & she is already swoln up with it & likely diseased too God grant it. He was so fair a child & I did like to play cross with him & touch him after to make him laugh. Did I tell you once he fell in the river & was no more than 6 or 7 & I made him take off his clothes & stand naked by the fire & he was shaking & ashamed & the next day brought me *piñones* from the hills?

Why have you not sent me the razor & strop & a little money? I looked forward to it. The blade I have as I told you is of little use & I have only a piece of cow leather & it full of thicknesses & sores. I can make no edge upon it & so much abuse my face & am obliged to make a poor soap out of roots. Surely it is a mean thing to ask & I suppose you set yourself up there as my benefactor do you? You covet me my place with Him & do seek therefore to purchase a good word from me. Be uncertain of my good intercession brother until you have piled on your account. I have friends & patrons before you be assured & they have some better claim & to be true I scarce can get you in. You had better think hard on it your need & mine. Confide in me if it be so that Catherine does speak ill of me. It returns on you & your children. I think she does slander me round about but you can tell me the nature of it & I will bless you outside of it & know you my best brother & my friend. You know I have the way of saving you. I have studied on it for a long time tho' it is truly a most difficult thing but after all nothing to me.

Some days He comes to me in a sourceless light that rises on His image at my bed & then I am caught of it & shine also as with lightning on me. I think He does console me but I am not consoled tho' I much want it—more than all things other. He does bid me speak all my love but I cannot for I am always just then under it the whole heft of it & am mute against it as against a little mountain heaved upon me & can utter no help of the thing that is done to me. Yet I can hear it in me the cry that is lain upon & stopped in me & I wonder after that He is gone that He was not even there. Thus does He chide me & I take some humor in it for surely I would not be lost &

scolded too. You can see that it is so. You can see it that
there is no doubt of it at all. Would you favor me with
this witness that you can see it? It is no matter to me of
course why should it be but I would have you say it to be
certain you think aright & are not in the least deceived.
This much I owe to you to see that you reckon rightly
upon this & other matters which affect your soul.

O I am pleased to hear from you whatever news you
can impart & do not neglect to tell me 1 little part of it the
things you & your good family entertain. I like to ponder
it & lay my blessings upon it with all good will. Welcome
& share with yours the fond & sincere offices of

Your humble brother,
N.V.

Father Olguin was consoled now that he had seen to
the saint's heart. This was what he had been waiting
for, a particular glimpse of his own ghost, a small,
innocuous ecstasy. He was troubled, too, of course; he
had that obligation. But he had been made the gift, as
it were, of another man's sanctity, and it would accom-
modate him very well. He replaced the letter and closed
the book. He could sleep now, and tomorrow he would
become a figure, an example in the town. In among
them, he would provide the townspeople with an order
of industry and repose. He closed his good eye; the
other was cracked open and dull in the yellow light; the
ball was hard and opaque, like a lump of frozen mar-
row in the bone.

When Angela returned that night to the Benevides
house, she was alive to the black silent world of the
canyon. The roadsides rushed through her vision in a
torrent of gray-white shapes like hailstones coming forever and too fast from the highest reach of the head-
lights, down and away to nothingness in the black
wake. She drove on, and she was sensible of creating
the wind at her window out of the cold black stillness
that lay against the walls of the canyon. Something she
bore down upon and passed, a bobcat or a fox, before
it sprang away, fixed her in its queer, momentary gaze,

its round eyes full of the bright reflection of the lights and burning on in her vision for a time afterward, brighter than an animal's eyes, brighter at last than the windows of the Benevides house, which mirrored her slow approach and stop. And there was the dying of the wind she had made, and of the motor and the light itself. And in her getting out and straining to see, there was no longer a high white house of stucco and stone, looming out against the leaves of the orchard, but a black organic mass the night had heaved up, even as long ago the canyon itself had been wrenched out of time, delineated in red and white and purple rock, lost each day out of its color and shape, and only the awful, massive presence of it remained, and the silence. It was no longer the chance place of her visitation, or the tenth day, but now the dominion of her next day and the day after, as far ahead as she cared to see. In the morning she would look at the Benevides house from the road, from her walk along the river, while eating an orange or imagining that she could feel, ever so little, the motion of life within her. She would see into the windows and the doors, and she would know the arrangement of her days and hours in the upstairs and down, and they would be for her the proof of her being and having been. She would see whether the hollyhocks were bent with bees and the eaves loud with birds. She would regard the house in the light of day. In fact it was secret like herself, the Benevides house. That was its peculiar character, that like a tomb it held the world at bay. She could clear her throat within, or scream and be silent. And the Benevides house, which she had seen from the river and the road, to which she had made claim by virtue of her regard, this house would be the wings and the stage of a reckoning. There were crickets away in the blackness.

JULY 28

The canyon is a ladder to the plain. The valley is pale in the end of July, when the corn and melons come of age and slowly the fields are made ready for the yield, and a faint, false air of autumn—an illusion still in the land—rises somewhere away in the high north country, a vague suspicion of red and yellow on the farthest summits. And the town lies out like a scattering of bones in the heart of the land, low in the valley, where the earth is a kiln and the soil is carried here and there in the wind and all harvests are a poor survival of the seed. It is a remote place, and divided from the rest of the world by a great forked range of mountains on the north and west; by wasteland on the south and east, a region of dunes and thorns and burning columns of air; and more than these by time and silence.

There is a kind of life that is peculiar to the land in summer—a wariness, a seasonal equation of well-being and alertness. Road runners take on the shape of motion itself, urgent and angular, or else they are like the gnarled, uncovered roots of ancient, stunted trees, some ordinary ruse of the land itself, immovable and forever there. And quail, at evening, just failing to suggest the waddle of too much weight, take cover with scarcely any talent for alarm, and spread their wings to the ground; and if then they are made to take flight, the imminence of no danger on earth can be more apparent; they explode away like a shot, and there is nothing but the dying whistle and streak of their going. Frequently in the sun there are pairs of white and russet hawks soaring to the hunt. And when one falls off and alights, there will be a death in the land, for it has come down to place itself like a destiny between its prey and the burrow from which its prey has come; and then the other, the killer hawk, turns around in the sky and breaks its glide and dives. It is said that hawks, when they have nothing to fear in the open land, dance upon the warm carnage of their kills. In the highest heat of the day, rattlesnakes lie outstretched upon the dunes, as if the sun had wound them out and lain upon them like a line of fire, or, knowing of some vibrant presence on the air, they writhe away in the agony of time. And of their own accord they go at sundown into the earth, hopelessly, as if to some unimaginable reckoning in the underworld. Coyotes have the gift of being seldom seen; they keep to the edge of vision and beyond, loping in and out of cover on the plains and highlands. And at night, when the whole world belongs to them, they parley at the river with the dogs, their higher, sharper voices full of authority and rebuke. They are an old council of clowns, and they are listened to.

Higher, among the hills and mesas and sandstone cliffs, there are foxes and bobcats and mountain lions. Now and then, when the weather turns and food is scarce in the mountains, bear and deer wander down into the canyons. Once there were wolves in the mountains, and the old hunters of the town remember them. It is said that they were many, and they came to the hunters' fires at night and sat around in the dark timber like old men wanting to smoke. But they were killed out for bounty, and no one will remember them in a little while. Great golden eagles nest among the highest outcrops of rock on the mountain peaks. They are sacred, and one of them, a huge female, old and burnished, is kept alive in a cage in the town. Even so, deprived of the sky, the eagle soars in man's imagination; there is divine malice in the wild eyes, an unmerciful intent. The eagle ranges far and wide over the land, farther than any other creature, and all things there are related simply by having existence in the perfect vision of a bird.

These—and the innumerable meaner creatures, the

lizard and the frog, the insect and the worm—have tenure in the land. The other, latecoming things—the beasts of burden and of trade, the horse and the sheep, the dog and the cat—these have an alien and inferior aspect, a poverty of vision and instinct, by which they are estranged from the wild land, and made tentative. They are born and die upon the land, but then they are gone away from it as if they had never been. Their dust is borne away in the wind, and their cries have no echo in the rain and the river, the commotion of wings, the return of boughs bent by the passing of dark shapes in the dawn and dusk.

Man came down the ladder to the plain a long time ago. It was a slow migration, though he came only from the caves in the canyons and the tops of the mesas nearby. There are low, broken walls on the tabletops and smoke-blackened caves in the cliffs, where still there are metates and broken bowls and ancient ears of corn, as if the prehistoric civilization had gone out among the hills for a little while and would return; and then everything would be restored to an older age, and time would have returned upon itself and a bad dream of invasion and change would have been dissolved in an hour before the dawn. For man, too, has tenure in the land; he dwelt upon the land twenty-five thousand years ago, and his gods before him.

The people of the town have little need. They do not hanker after progress and have never changed their essential way of life. Their invaders were a long time in conquering them; and now, after four centuries of Christianity, they still pray in Tanoan to the old deities of the earth and sky and make their living from the things that are and have always been within their reach; while in the discrimination of pride they acquire from their conquerors only the luxury of example. They have assumed the names and gestures of their enemies, but have held on to their own, secret souls; and in this there is a resistance and an overcoming, a long outwaiting.

Abel walked into the canyon. His return to the town

had been a failure, for all his looking forward. He had tried in the days that followed to speak to his grandfather, but he could not say the things he wanted; he had tried to pray, to sing, to enter into the old rhythm of the tongue, but he was no longer attuned to it. And yet it was there still, like memory, in the reach of his hearing, as if Francisco or his mother or Vidal had spoken out of the past and the words had taken hold of the moment and made it eternal. Had he been able to say it, anything of his own language—even the commonplace formula of greeting "Where are you going"—which had no being beyond sound, no visible substance, would once again have shown him whole to himself; but he was dumb. Not dumb—silence was the older and better part of custom still—but *inarticulate*.

He quit the pavement where it rose and wound upon a hill, suddenly very much relieved to be alone in the sunlit canyon, going on in his long easy stride by the slow, shining river, the water cool and shallow and clear on the sand. He followed with his eyes the converging parallel rims of the canyon walls, deepening in the color of distance until they gave way to the wooded mountains looming on the sky. There were huge clouds flaring out and sailing low with water above the Valle Grande. And, stopping once to drink from the river, he turned around and saw the valley below, a great pool of the sunlit sky, and red and purple hills; and here and upward from this height to the top of the continent the air was distilled to the essence of summer and noon, and nothing lay between the object and the eye.

He began almost to be at peace, as if he had drunk a little of warm, sweet wine, for a time no longer centered upon himself. He was alone, and he wanted to make a song out of the colored canyon, the way the women of Torreón made songs upon their looms out of colored yarn, but he had not got the right words together. It would have been a creation song; he would have sung lowly of the first world, of fire and flood, and of the emergence of dawn from the hills. And had he brought food to eat along the way, he would have wanted it to be a crust of oven bread, heavy and moist, pitted with cinders and ash, or a blue cornmeal cake full of grit and sweet smoke.

The noon hour passed, and part of the next, and he was below and across the road from an old copper mine, a ghost, too, like the ancient towns that lay upon the ridge above and behind him, given up to the consuming earth and left alone amid the remnants of some old and curious haste: broken implements, red and eaten through with rust; charred and rotting wood; a thousand pieces of clear and green and amber glass upon the swollen ground, as if untold legions of ants had come to raise a siegeworks at Alesia. The black face of the shaft, higher on the slope but not yet so high as the base of the sunlit cliff, there in its gray wooden frame, reminded him of something. It was deeper than shade, and he knew without looking that no cave or crevice in the opposite wall was like it, no other thing in the canyon was so sharply defined. He turned his eyes away from it and saw again the running water and the light upon it and here and there the bits of drift that bobbed and hung among the stones. Farther on he came upon a rise and saw the settlement at the springs, the corrugated iron roofs gleaming, the bright orchards, and the high white walls of the Benevides house. He hurried on.

Angela Grace St. John sat in the downstairs and waited for him to come. She had waited for days, without caring how many, among the lines of light in the rooms. These were a labyrinth of colors in the afternoon, a glowing on the mouths of pitchers and jars, and somber glare upon the polish of porcelain and wood. She listened. There are sounds that do not designate anything in particular, and for that reason go unheard: water dripping from a faucet and the drone of bees, long steady labor out of sight. There was a tractor in the field across the road, moving slowly back and forth upon a stand of hay. She had awakened to the sound of it, but it had begun a long time before she

awoke, and now it was going on long after she had
ceased to hear, every thousand hollow strokes of the
engine echoing out and away from the land. Then she
heard the sudden swing of the gate, and she knew that
it was he. Just then she had no need to see him, and she
sat still, listening. He worked more rapidly than before
and with a certain slight exaggeration of his strength:
four and sometimes five and six slanting strokes of the
axe, hurried and uneven, then the pause and the spinning away of the chips and the length of wood striking
easily upon the pile and clattering down, and at the
same time the friction of another log upon the block.

Later, when shade rose up in the canyon and the
long false dusk came about, she had to get out. She
locked the doors and walked along the road to the
bathhouse. The attendant said nothing, but laid out the
towels in one of the stalls and drew the tub full of
smoking mineral water. Angela closed the curtains, undressed, and lay down in the water. After a while she
went limp, and she could hear only her own slow,
steady breathing and, with it, the water lapping. She
sighed all of her strength away and laid her head back
against the rim of the tub. Like drift almost, her limbs
rose and rocked in the steaming water. Her feet and the
caps of her knees were red with heat. She felt the clean,
warm beads of water rising out upon her brow, standing, then running down her temples and into the towel
that held her hair. She was glad to lose track of the
time, glad of drifting into mindlessness, of holding off
for an hour the vague presentiment of shame that
lurked within her. Later she lay down upon a table and
the attendant wrapped her in light cotton blankets and
she dozed.

When she returned to the Benevides house, Abel was
sitting on the front stoop—not waiting, it seemed—still
and stolid. The last line of light had risen to the rim of
the canyon wall, and even then it was dying out upon
the blood-red rock above the trees. The enormous dark
that filled the canyon was strangely cold, colder by far
than the night would be. Half of the pale moon lay

upon the skyline. A hummingbird swung slowly back and forth at the bunch of bridal veil under the eaves. The bees had not yet gone away.

He followed her silently into the house and through the dark rooms. She turned on the light in the kitchen, and the sudden burst of it made her shrink ever so little. She gave him coffee and he sat listening to her, not waiting, gently taking hold of her distress, passing it off. She was grateful—and chagrined. She had not foreseen this turn of tables and events, had not imagined that he could turn her scheme around. She had meant to be amused, but as it was she was only grateful and chagrined. What struck her most, and held her pride intact, was the merest compulsion to laugh, not the derision that she might have intended but a cold, uneasy mirth—and the slightest fear—now taking shape within her. Before her now was the strange reality of her shame and the tyranny of light that lay upon it. She was not herself, her own idea of herself, disseminating and at ease. She had no will to shrug him off. He sat looking at her, not waiting, still and easy upon some instinct, some sense or other of dominion and desire. She hovered about the hard flame of it.

When she polished the cup and saucer and replaced them in the cupboard, Angela's breath was short and uneven. "All right," she said faintly, and she sighed. The "all right" was neither consent nor resignation, just something to say. She had hoped that he might say something, too, anything of his own accord; it should have made everything so much easier. But he said nothing.

"Abel," she said after a moment, "do you think that I am beautiful?"

She had gone to the opposite wall and turned. She leaned back with her hands behind her, throwing her head a little in order to replace a lock of hair that had fallen across her brow. She sucked at her cheeks, musing.

"No, not beautiful," he said.

"Would you like to make love to me?"

"Yes."

She looked evenly at him, no longer musing.

"You really would, wouldn't you? Yes. God, I've seen the way you look at me sometimes."

There was no reaction from him.

"And do you imagine," she went on, "that *I* would like it, too?"

"I don't know," he answered, "but I imagine you would."

Angela caught her breath, and after a long moment she came to him. She bent down and kissed him, and he put his hands on her and drew her close against him. She felt the strength of his hands and the heat of his body. His hands were hard with work and sharp with the odor of wood. She took hold of one of his hands.

She led him through the rooms and up the stairs quickly, quietly. The corridor was dark, but there was a night light in her room. The room was warm and full of great soft shadows. She let go of his hand and turned away to undress. He could see her reflection, like a silhouette, in an oval mirror on the wall. When she faced him again, they were both naked. For a minute they stood still in the soft blue light. Abel studied her, but she did not cringe. She was very pale in her nakedness, and slight. But her body was supple and round. Her throat was long and her shoulders narrow and tapered. Her breasts were small and rather too low on her body, but they were firm and pointed. There was a soft curve to her belly, and her thighs flared from the hips. Her legs were slim and shapely; she was wide between the legs.

"What will you do to me?" she asked. She was heaving a little, and her mouth was soft and open. Her face and throat were delicately beautiful against the black of her hair.

They came together and Angela felt with her whole body that he was lean and hard and vital, that his dark skin was warm and wet and taut with excitement. She felt the muscles of his stomach and thighs roll and crawl upon her, and she gasped. He let her down very gently on the bed and lay over her. He kissed her forehead and her eyes and her open mouth, and the weight of his shoulders and chest bore slowly down upon her until it seemed to her that she should soon be crushed beneath him.

"*All right*," she said again, quickly and without breath.

"No, not yet," he said, and for an instant she went limp and the edge of her desire was lost. Oh no, *oh no!* she thought, but he knew what he was doing. His tongue and the tips of his fingers were everywhere upon her, and he brought her back so slowly, and set such awful fire to her flesh, that she wanted to scream. At last he raised up and she set herself for him. She was moaning softly, and her eyes rolled. He was dark and massive above her, poised and tinged with pale blue light. And in that split second she thought again of the badger at the water, and the great bear, blue-black and blowing.

As always in summer, the moment at which evening had come upon the town was absolute and imperceptible. And out of the town, among the hills and fields, the shadows had grown together and taken hold of the dusk until the valley itself was a soft gray shadow. Even so, there was a great range of colors within it, more various even than the sky, which now had begun to blush and fade. And the tinted rocks and soils grew supple and soft, and the shine went off the leaves.

Whispers rose up among the rows of corn, and the old man rested for a moment, bent still with his hands to the hoe. For nearly an hour now he had not been able to see well into the furrows, and he had reckoned their depth by the feel of the blade against the earth and made them true by the touch of the fronds and tassels on his neck and arms. The sweat dried up on his neck and the mud dried at his feet, and still he rested, holding off for another moment the pain of straightening his fingers and his back. At last he raised up against the stiffness in his spine, gathering the crippled leg under him. He breathed out sharply with the effort, and at the same time unlocked his hands and let the handle of the hoe fall into the crook of his arm. There was a lot of work left to do; he must yet bend again to the fetlocks of the mares, and his fingers must slip the hobbles from the hoofs; must yet lay hold of the wagon tongue and the buckles and stays of the harness, twice, even; must then carry water to the trough and cleave the portions from the bale. But he didn't think of that; he thought instead of coffee and bread and the dark interior of his room.

But *were* they whispers? Something there struck beneath the level of his weariness, struck and took hold in his hearing like the cry of a small creature—a field mouse or a young rabbit. Evening gives motion to the air, and the long blades of corn careen and collide, and there is always at dusk the rustling of leaves that settle into night. But was it that? All day his mind had wandered over the past, habitually, beyond control and even the least notion of control, but his thoughts had been by some slight strand of attention anchored to his work. The steady repetition of his backward steps—the flash of the hoe and the sure advance of the brown water after it—had been a small reality from which his mind must venture and return. But now, at the end of long exertion, his aged body let go of the mind, and he was suddenly conscious of some alien presence close at hand. And he knew as suddenly, too, that it had been there for a long time, not approaching, but impending for minutes, and even hours, upon the air and the growth and the land around. He held his breath and listened. His ears rang with weariness; beyond that there was nothing save the soft sound of water and wind and, somewhere among the farthest rows, the momentary scuttle of a quail; then the low whistle and blowing of the mares in the adjacent field, reminding him of the time. But there was something else; something apart from these, not quite absorbed into the ordinary silence: an excitement of breathing in the in-

stant just past, all ways immediate, irrevocable even
now that it had ceased to be. He peered into the dark
rows of corn from which no sound had come, in which
no presence was. There was only the deep black wall of
stalks and leaves, vibrating slowly upon his tired vision
like water. He was too old to be afraid. His acknowl-
edgment of the unknown was nothing more than a dull,
intrinsic sadness, a vague desire to weep, for evil had
long since found him out and knew who he was. He set
a blessing upon the corn and took up his hoe. He
shuffled out between the rows, toward the dim light at
the edge of the cornfield.

And where he had stood the water backed up in the
furrow and spilled over the edge. It spread out upon
the ground and filled the double row of crescents where
the heels of his shoes had pressed into the earth. Here
and there were the black welts of mud which he had
shaken loose from the blade of the hoe. And there the
breathing resumed, rapid and uneven with excitement.
Above the open mouth, the nearly sightless eyes followed the old man out of the cornfield, and the barren
lids fluttered helplessly behind the colored glass.

AUGUST 1

Three days passed, and Father Olguin went about his work as usual. These full summer days he breathed more peacefully the cool, musky air of the rectory, gathered himself up privately in the mornings after Mass, when his blood was always slow to thaw and his mind to focus and take hold of events. By the grace of these last few days, the affairs of the parish had been set in order. He was content. He had at last begun to sense the rhythm of life in the ancient town, and how it was that his own pulse should eventually conform to it. And this in itself was a grave satisfaction to him. He had always been on the lookout for reverences, and here was a holiness more intrinsic than any he could ever have imagined—a slow, druidic procession of seasons in the narrow streets.

Now, on the first day of August, there was a stirring in the town. Fewer men than usual went out into the fields, and the women scurried about like squirrels, full of chatter, inside and out, from door to door. There was a curious sound of deliberation and haste all around. Embers and ashes rose up on the shimmering columns of heat above the mud ovens, whirled, and settled into the streets, and the sharp odor of cedar and gumwood smoke carried to the edge of the town and beyond, into the still midmorning of the valley. And there, southward on the old road to San Ysidro, the first covered wagons had come into view. In these were the outriding elders of the caravan, an older generation of the *Dîné* than that which followed and would follow through the afternoon and evening, and which even now convened at the junction to trade for wine. All afternoon the wagons would come from the south,

65

slowly, seemingly motionless on the steady grade, but looming larger until at last the great gray canopies ballooned like sails taking shape in the distant plain, and in the angle of the wake on either side lean young men on horseback, drab and drunk; the beautiful straight-backed girls in sunlit silver and velveteen, supple and slim and born to the saddle; and the panting dogs. Later, when their chores were done, the children of the town would run out to see, to stand at the fences and cheer and chide; there would be an old enactment of laughter and surprise. The end of the train would be brought up by fools, in a poor parody of pride: the fat, degenerate squaws, insensible with drink, and the sad, sullen bucks, hanging on. But these now in view were clansmen, the wizened keepers of an old and sacred alliance, come to prolong for another year the agony of recognition and retreat.

Later, when Father Olguin had taken honey from the hives and heard the general clamor rise above the drone of the bees, he thought of Angela. He could do so now without the small excitement that she had so easily provoked within him at first. He was aware of her as a woman, of course, but he was no longer disturbed by her. Tacitly, as it were, she had agreed to keep her distance. How else could her silence be construed? She was capable of respect. Very well, then, he would repay her in kind; he would extend to her his welcome at once, now, upon this certain occasion of grave good will. Unaccustomed as she was to solitude—lonely, no doubt—she would share in his good fortune simply, implicitly. She would *perceive* that he was occupied, committed surely to a remarkable trust, and she would envy him—not his accomplishment, perhaps, but at least his possibilities. The prospect of her envy pleased him, and he hummed about in the rooms of the rectory until it was noon, and he rang the Angelus long and loud.

The general sound did not diminish after noon, when ordinarily the weight of silence lay most heavily on the town, but went on, gathering momentum. The customary motion of the day had been suspended, and he had the sense of an impending revolution in time, as if a new, more crowded order of events were about to be imposed upon the world. Nor did the premonition subside when, almost reluctantly, he drove out of the town and into the canyon, leaving behind the din of the coming feast. A strange exuberance had taken hold of him, a low exhilaration like fire; he breathed softly upon it and opened his hand to the force of the air outside.

A low line of thunderheads lay on the high horizon in back of the northernmost peaks. They were deep in the distance and seemed always to have been there, dark and unchanging in the end of vision, in some sense polar and nocturnal. He kept an eye on them and speeded up, half hoping to rush upon the scent of rain. The specter of rain in August is a distillation of light upon the land, a harder efflorescence upon the rocks and a sterile, uncommon shine upon the river and the leaves. An element of darkness, however vague and tentative on the midsummer sky, implies a thin and colorless luster upon the sand and the cliffs and the dusty boughs of cedar and pine, and there is a quality like vain resistance in the air.

The roof and walls of the Benevides house gleamed in the sun. He touched the brake and turned off the road into the white gravel driveway, in which there were drab patches of hard earth and protruding gray ridges of rock, too deeply embedded to be removed. The incline to the steps of the porch was uneven, and the gravel rolled backward under his sandaled feet. There were more flies than usual about the porch, and the vine cover rang with bees. Angela opened the door and nodded him in without speaking, smiling faintly in that way of hers that meant she was, or had just been, lost in her thoughts. Had he been in the least suspicious, he might have seen that she was startled, however little, to see him, and been aware of a certain oppressive stillness about her. As it was, he came into the dark room, in which all the shades were drawn, and sat down. He made himself comfortable, at home. They were making ready in the town, he said, like dervishes. She should see.

From the first he presumed to approach her officiously, on the basis of his own prejudices: a jealousy for Aesop and the ring of Genesis, an instinctive demand upon all histories to be fabulous. Thus he went on for several minutes. The town, he said—though not in so many words—observed an old and solar calendar, upon which were fixed the advents and passiontides of all deities, the last, least whisper of all oracles, the certain days and years of all damnation and deliverance. She listened. She listened through him to the sound of thunder and of rain that fell upon the mountain miles away, that split open the sky and set an awful tremor on the trees. She heard the touch of rain upon the cones of evergreen spines, heard even the laden boughs bending and the panes of water that rose and ran upon the black slopes. And this while he spoke and the heat of drought lay outside upon the windows and the walls. She had a craving for the rain. Her eyes smarted for it, and the lines of her mouth deepened. Directly he fell silent, aware of her behind him. He turned and looked at her for the first time. She seemed very small in the dark room. He waited for her to speak. " 'Oh my God,' " she said, laughing. " 'I am heartily sorry . . . for having offended Thee.' " She laughed. It was hard and brittle, her laughter, but far from desperate, underlain with perfect presence, nearly too controlled. And that, even more than the meaning and the mockery, horrified him. He stiffened. There was nothing then but her voice in the room, going on wearily, without inflection, even after he had ceased to hear.

Afterward, when Father Olguin returned to the town, the streets were filled with people. Children shouted to him and animals darted in front of the car, chickens and dogs and sheep. He drove down upon them and they scattered. He leaned on the horn and swerved. Out of the corner of his good eye he saw a child leap out of the way and fall. The child rolled over and laughed. Suddenly the walls of the town rang out with laughter and enclosed him all around. He turned here and there into the streets, and the streets led only to an endless succession of steep earthen walls, and the walls were lined with people, innumerable and grotesque. Everywhere he caught sight of men and women, bloated or shriveled up with age, children running and writhing on the sheer tide of revelry; and a sameness of distance upon all their eyes, their one timeless enigmatic face constrained into idiocy and delight. Fear and revulsion jarred upon his brain. The car lunged under him, veered sharply around a blind corner of walls, and the tire nearest him lay over upon itself and the sharp edge of the tread blasted the sand of the street into the metal about and beneath him; and there, directly before him, were the high covered hoops of a wagon, the iron bands of the wheels and the small black cavern of its depth. He slammed on the brakes and heard the tires slice and fold into the sand and lock upon the packed earth. He felt the whip of momentum pass through him, the enormous weight of motion that fell upon the engine and drove it down on the coils. Then in the ebbing pitch and rock that followed, as the cloud of dust and laughter drew down upon him, he saw the cradleboard fixed to the wagon. And just above and beyond the bobbing ornament of the hood, at the level of his own eyes, was the face of the infant inside. Its little eyes were overhung with fat, and its cheeks and chins sagged down in front of the tight swaddle at its throat. The hair lay in tight wet rings above the eyes, and all the shapeless flesh of the face dripped with sweat and shone like copper in the sunlight. Flies crawled upon the face and lay thick about the eyes and mouth. The muscles twitched under the fat and the head turned slowly from side to side in the agony of sad and helpless laughter. Then the wall of dust de-

scended upon the face, and the cries of the children
became a shrill and incessant chant: "Padre! Padre!
Padre!"

Thunder cracked in the sky and rolled upon the
mountains. It grew deep and filled the funnel of the
canyon and reverberated endlessly upon the cliffs.
Lightning flashed, rending the dark wall of rain, casting
an awful glare on it, and the rain moved into the
canyon, almost slowly, upon the warm and waning
gusts of drought, and the golden margin of receding
light grew pale in the mist. And there behind the squall
the still-invisible torrents coming on, like the sound of a
great turbine, the roar of the wind and the rain on the
river and the rocks, the heavy drift borne up and set
loose to spin into the pools and collide on the banks,
and the faint falling apart of the earth itself, breaking
and shifting under the weight of water.

The wind rose up under the eaves, and the rooms of
the Benevides house quaked and grew black. Angela
drew herself up and waited. The intermittent drops of
rain upon the roof seemed almost to subside; then the
first great slanting sheets of water drove against the
gutter and ascended the north wall; it beat down on the
windows and the eaves like hail and set a deafening roar
on the iron roof. So sudden and loud was the descent of
storm that she dug her nails into the heels of her hands
and cowered instinctively. She arched her throat and
her eyes glanced upward to the dark ceiling and source
of so much sound. The intense wake of the sound
engulfed her and she flung open the door and looked
out. She could hear only the roar of the rain and the
peal of thunder, breaking low and overhead in the
hanging darkness. She could see only the flashes of
lightning and the awful gray slant of the flood, pale and
impenetrable, splintering upon itself and cleaving her
vision like pain. The first, fast wave of the storm passed
with scarcely any abatement of sound; the troughs at
the eaves filled and flowed, and the thick ropes of water

hung down among the hollyhocks and mint and ate away the earth at their roots; the glaze of rain water rose up among the clean white stones and ran in panels on the road; and across the road the rumble and rush of the river. And again the wind rose up and the thunder struck and the rain leaned out across the canyon. It drove into the open end of the porch like shot and glanced off her bare legs. At the source of the rain the deep black bank of the sky swelled and roiled, moving slowly southward, under the rock rims of the canyon walls. And in the cold and denser dark, with the sound and sight of the fury all around, Angela stood transfixed in the open door and breathed deep into her lungs the purest electric scent of the air. She closed her eyes, and the clear aftervision of the rain, which she could still hear and feel so perfectly as to conceive of nothing else, obliterated all the mean and myriad fears that had laid hold of her in the past. Sharpest angles of light played on the lids of her eyes, and the great avalanche of sound fell about her.

The feasting had begun, and there was a lull on the town. The crippled old man in leggings and white ceremonial trousers shuffled out into the late afternoon. He dried his eyes on his sleeve and whimpered one last time in his throat. He was grown too old, he thought. He could not understand what had happened. But even his sorrow was feeble now; it had withered, like his leg, over the years, and only once in a while, when something unusual happened to remind him of it, did it take on the edge and point of pain. So it was that as he made his way along toward the Middle and smelled the food and fires of the feast, he wondered what his sorrow was and could not remember. Still the wagons came, and he heard in the distance the occasional laughter which brought them in. It had the sound of weariness now, and it rose up less frequently. It would soon be time for the Pecos bull to appear, and the smaller children made ready to attend. Out of the doorways he passed came the queer, halting talk of old fellowship, Tanoan and Athapascan, broken English and Spanish. He smelled the odor of boiled coffee, and it was good. He cared less for the sweet smell of piki and the moist, broken loaves of sotobalau, the hot spicy odors of paste and posole; for old men do not hunger much. Better for their novelty were the low open fires of the wagon camps, the sweet fat which dripped and sizzled on the embers, the burned, roasted mutton, and the fried bread. And more delicious than these was the laden air that carried the smoke and drew it out in long thin lines above the roofs, swelling in advance of the rain. The immense embankment of the storm had blackened out the whole horizon to the north. The compressed density of its core, like a great black snake writhing, drew out of the mouth of the canyon, recoiled upon the warm expanse of the valley, and resumed the slow, sure approach upon the intervening gullies and hills and fields above the town. And the old man had an ethnic, planter's love of harvests and of rain. And just there on the obsidian sky, extending out and across the eastern slope of the plain, was a sheer and perfect arc of brilliant colors.

It made him glad to be in the midst of talk and celebration, to savor the rich relief of the coming rain upon the rows of beans and chilies and corn, to see the return of weather, of trade and reunion upon the town. He tossed his head in greeting to the shy Navajo children who hid among the camps and peered, afraid of his age and affliction. For they, too, were a harvest, in some intractable sense the regeneration of his own bone and blood. The *Diné,* of all people, knew how to be beautiful. Here and there in the late golden light which bled upon the walls, he saw the bright blankets and the gleaming silverwork of their wealth: the shining weight of their buckles and belts, bracelets and bow guards, squash blossoms and pale blue stones. Had he anything at all of value, he would have liked to barter for such a stone, a great oval spider web, like a robin's egg, to wear upon his hand. And he would have been shrewd and indifferent; he would certainly have had the better of it. Such a stone was medicine, they said; it could preserve the sight. It could restore an old man's vision. They sang about it, he supposed, and no wonder, no wonder.

He turned in to the Middle and the holy place. The shrine for Porcingula, Our Lady of the Angels, had been raised at the center of the north side and adjacent to the kiva. It was a small green enclosure, a framework of wood and wire, covered with boughs of cedar and pine. He bowed before it, though as yet there was nothing but the bare altar and the benches inside. Tomorrow it would be made beautiful with candles and cloth and holy with incense. He would see to it, for he was the sacristan, after all. Two young boys would stand with rifles at the open side, and he would remind them of their trust. And after Mass the lovely Lady would be borne in procession from the church, and the little horse would come to greet her in the aisle, would precede her out into the Campo Santo and dance beside her in the streets; and the bull would lope all around and wheel and hook the air with its wooden horns, and the black-faced children, who were the invaders, and the clowns would follow, laughing and taunting with curses, upon its heels. The Lady would stand all day in her shrine, and the governor and his officials would sit in attendance at her feet, and one by one the dancers of the squash and turquoise clans would appear on top of the kiva, coming out upon the sky in their rich ceremonial dress, descend the high ladder to the earth, and kneel before her.

He took hold of the smooth poles and raised himself slowly up the rungs of the ladder, careful to place the crooked leg just so, where, if his weight should shift on it, the bone itself would suffice like a cane to hold him up. But it was a nearly empty precaution, not against his strength so much but against some element of doubt and fear that had lately come upon him like the shadow of his old age. His arms and hands were strong, and his shoulders bunched at the back of his neck and made a deep groove of his spine. He crept closer to the high

vertical wall of the kiva, pressing the whole surface of
his body against the slanting poles and rungs of the
ladder, so that even the weight of his chest and shoulders amounted to nothing almost and there was no
center to it; at last he laid his cheek on the final rung
and saw the gray warp of the wood where the sun had
dried and split it open and the red metal winding which
spliced it to the poles and cut into it and stained it with
rust. Then, without looking, could he reach upward and
take hold of the wall itself. He drew himself over the
top and stood for a moment to catch his breath. The
rain had overtaken the hills above the town and the sky
grew dark overhead. He felt the whirlwinds which ran
upon the roofs and heard the distant bleating and lowing of the livestock, milling about on the weather's
edge. And under him the great rafters of the kiva
vibrated with the sound of thunder and drums. He
looked south and west in the direction of the sunlit
fields; they lay out like patchwork in the pool of light;
and beyond, the black line of the mesa was edged with
light. He let himself down into the great earthen
darkness of the room.

When he emerged with the other holy men out of the
kiva, it was dusk and the rain had begun to fall in the
streets, unevenly at first, spotting and pitting the dust
with dark, round stains; then it grew fine and steady,
and the hard earth of the Middle began to shine. The
people had come out of doors, and they stood about,
waiting in the rain. He drew his blanket around him
and went with the others to the house from which the
little horse was now made ready to come. When they
got to the doorway, he opened the screen and the horse
began to dance. The collar of tin shells began to trem-
ble with sound, and at the same time the drummer
began the incessant roll and rattle of the sticks upon the
drum. The little horse emerged into the dim light and
the rain, and the drummer and the old men followed.
The horse was an ancient likeness, like the black Arabi-
an of the Moors, its head too small and finely wrought
and the arch of its throat too severe. But it was a

beautiful sensitive thing, and the dancer gave it life.
The spotted hide was taut and smooth on the frame,
and the framework rode hard and low on the dancer's
waist. It was he who gave it motion and mystery. He
was dressed all in black, and under the bright kilt
which hung from the shoulders and haunches of the
little horse his black boots minced upon the earth,
moving too little and too fast to follow. And his body
and the body of the little horse were set in high, nervous agitation, like a leaf in the stiff wind. But all the
strange and violent tremor ceased at his head, and he
seemed to be standing there, perfectly still and apart,
mindless and invisible behind the veil. And the black
hat and the black mask of the flowing veil, which lay in
the wind and rain upon the bones of the face, made a
dark and motionless silhouette upon the dusk, and the
blur of motion under it gave it sheer relief.

The medicine men presided over the little horse with
prayers and plumes, pollen and meal. And elsewhere in
the streets, approaching on a wave of sound, the bull
came running. The clowns were close upon it, and it
veered and drew up short and crouched, only to wheel
among them and run on. And the black-faced clowns
gave chase, shouting their obscene taunts, and the small
invaders, absurd in the parody of fear, grabbed at their
gored flesh and lay strewn about in the path of the
beast. And the bull was a sad and unlikely thing, a
crude and makeshift totem of revelry and delight.
There was no holiness to it, none of the centaur's sacred
mien and motion, but only the look of evil. It was a
large skeleton of wood, drawn over loosely with black
cloth upon which were painted numerous white rings
like brands. Its horns were a length of wood fixed hori-
zontally upon the sheepskin head; its eyes were black
metal buttons and its tongue a bit of faded red cloth.
But it was a hard thing to be the bull, for there was a
primitive agony to it, and it was a kind of victim, an
object of ridicule and hatred; and harder now that the
men of the town had relaxed their hold upon the ancient ways, had grown soft and dubious. Or they had

merely grown old. The old man heard the clamor of the
clowns. He knew without looking around that the bull
had come into the Middle, and it was at his back and
he could see it perfectly in his mind. He thought of
Mariano and of running. The rain and the cold reminded him of a time long ago when the flurries of snow
rose up in the dawn and his legs were hale and he ran
whole and perfectly toward the town. And once he,
too, had been the bull—twice or three times, perhaps.
He could not remember how many, but he could
remember that it was done honorably and well. He had
bent far forward and crouched with the likeness of the
bull on his back, the way he must, and even so, in the
angle of pain of that posture, he could have run away
forever from the clowns. But he must not think of that
now. The solemn little horse vibrated before him; the
veiled rider held its fine head high and its croup level,
never once relaxing the constant, nearly furious imposi-
tion of life upon it; the black mane and tail lay out in
commotion with the rain. The little horse moved here
and there among the elders of the town to be received
and anointed. The cacique spoke to it and sprinkled
meal upon it. And the townspeople and the visitors to
the town huddled in the rain and looked on. The bull
went running in the streets, and the clowns and the
antelope followed.

The rain diminished, and with nightfall the aftermath
of the storm moved slowly out upon the plain. The last
of the wagons had gone away from the junction, and
only three or four young Navajos remained at Paco's.
One of them had passed out and lay in his vomit on the
floor of the room. The others were silent now, and
sullen. They hung upon the bar and wheezed, helpless
even to take up the dregs of the wine that remained.
The precious ring of sweet red wine lay at the bottom
of a green quart bottle, and the dark convexity of the
glass rose and shone out of it like the fire of an emer-
ald. The green bottle lay out in the yellow glow of the
lamp, just there on the counter and within their reach.

They regarded it with helpless wonder. Abel and the white man paid no attention to them. The two spoke low to each other, carefully, as if the meaning of what they said was strange and infallible. Now and then the white man laughed, and each time it carried too high on the scale and ended in a strange, inhuman cry—as of pain. It was an old woman's laugh, thin and weak as water. It issued only from the tongue and teeth of the great evil mouth, and it fell away from the blue lips and there was nothing left of it. But the mouth hung open afterward and made no sound, and the great body quaked and the white hands jerked and trembled helplessly. The Navajos became aware of him. And throughout Abel smiled; he nodded and grew silent at length; and the smile was thin and instinctive, a hard, transparent mask upon his mouth and eyes. He waited, and the wine rose up in his blood.

And then they were ready, the two of them. They went out into the darkness and the rain. They crossed the highway and walked out among the dunes. The lights of the junction shone dim in the distance and wavered like candle flames in back of the swirling mist. When they were midway between the river and the road, they stopped. They were near a telegraph pole; it leaned upon the black sky and shone like coal. All around was silence, save for the sound of the rain and the moan of the wind in the wires. Abel waited. The white man raised his arms, as if to embrace him, and came forward. But Abel had already taken hold of the knife, and he drew it. He leaned inside the white man's arms and drove the blade up under the bones of the breast and across. The white man's hands lay on Abel's shoulders, and for a moment the white man stood very still. There was no expression on his face, neither rage nor pain, only the same translucent pallor and the vague distortion of sorrow and wonder at the mouth and invisible under the black glass. He seemed to look not at Abel but beyond, off into the darkness and the rain, the black infinity of sound and silence. Then he closed his hands upon Abel and drew him close. Abel heard the strange excitement of the white man's breath, and the quick, uneven blowing at his ear, and felt the blue shivering lips upon him, felt even the scales of the lips and the hot slippery point of the tongue, writhing. He was sick with terror and revulsion, and he tried to fling himself away, but the white man held him close. The white immensity of flesh lay over and smothered him. He withdrew the knife and thrust again, lower, deep into the groin. The whole strength of his arm and back lay into the slant of the blade across the bowels, and the flesh split open and the steaming gore fell out upon his hand. The white hands still lay upon him as if in benediction, and the awful gaze of the head, still fixed upon something beyond and behind him. Then the head inclined a little, as if to whisper something of the darkn ss and the rain, and the pale flesh of the face twitched, and the great blue mouth still gaped open and made no sound. The white hands laid hold of Abel and drew him close, and the terrible strength of the hands was brought to bear only in proportion as Abel resisted them. In his terror he knew only to wield the knife. He turned it upon the massive white arms and at last the white man's hands fell away from him, and he reeled backward and away, whimpering now, exhausted. Abel threw down the knife and the rain fell upon it and made it clean. When he looked up, the white man still was standing there, still intent upon some vision in the near distance, waiting. He seemed just then to wither and grow old. In the instant before he fell, his great white body grew erect and seemed to cast off its age and weight; it grew supple and sank slowly to the ground, as if the bones were dissolving within it. And Abel was no longer terrified, but strangely cautious and intent, full of wonder and regard. He could not think; there was nothing left inside him but a cold, instinctive will to wonder and regard. He approached and knelt down in the rain to watch death come upon the white man's face. He removed the little black glasses from the white man's face and laid them aside, carefully. At last the eyes of the white man's face curdled and were impervious to the rain. One of the arms lay out from the body; it was there, in the pale angle of the white man's death, that Abel knelt. The sleeve had been cut away, and the whole length of the arm and the open palm of the hand were exposed. The white, hairless arm shone like the underside of a fish, and the dark nails of the hand seemed a string of great black beads. He knelt over the white man for a long time in the rain, looking down.

AUGUST 2

There was the sound of the censer and the drum.
The procession of men and women wound out of the
church and through the streets. The statue rode high
upon the train and shone in the sun. The little horse
danced on the way, and the bull went running and
turning around. And the sun was high and the valley
shone and the fields were bright and clean after the
rain.

In a while the dancers filed out of the kiva. In two
long lines they danced, and the gourds and evergreen
boughs in their hands dipped and swayed to the sound
of the singing and the drums. Their feet fell upon the
earth in perfect time, and their eyes were solemn and
looked straight ahead. And the single deep voice of the
singers lay upon the dance, lay even upon the valley
and the earth, whole and inscrutable, everlasting.

"Abelito." The old man Francisco rode out in the
wagon to the fields. The lines lay low upon the flanks
of the mares, but the mares knew the way and they
went on their own to the river and the fields. The river
was high, and they drew the wagon into it and drank.
Without thinking, knowing only by instinct where he
was, the old man looked for the reed. It was there still,
but the rise of the river had reached it and made it
spring; it leaned out over the water, and the little noose
hung from it like a spider's thread.

And later, when he had got down from the wagon
and hobbled the mares, he carried his hoe into the rows
of corn. The corn was high, and the long blades glis-
tened in the sun. The harvest was all around him and
the tassels were dark and damp with the rain and the
great green ears were heavy and full of fragrance. He

could hear the distant sound of the drums and the deep, welling voice of the singers. He tried not to think of the dance, but it was there, going on in his brain. He could see the dancers perfectly in the mind's eye, could see even how they bowed and turned, where they were in relation to the walls and the doors and the slope of the earth. He had an old and infallible sense of what they were doing and had to do. Never before had he been away from the dance. "Abelito," he said again, and he began to hoe the rows. The long afternoon went on around him, and he was alone in the fields. He knew only that he was alone again.

2

THE PRIEST
OF THE SUN

Los Angeles, 1952

JANUARY 26

There is a small silversided fish that is found along the coast of southern California. In the spring and summer it spawns on the beach during the first three hours after each of the three high tides following the highest tide. These fishes come by the hundreds from the sea. They hurl themselves upon the land and writhe in the light of the moon, the moon, the moon; they writhe in the light of the moon. They are among the most helpless creatures on the face of the earth. Fishermen, lovers, passers-by catch them up in their bare hands.

The Priest of the Sun lived with his disciple Cruz on the first floor of a two-story red-brick building in Los Angeles. The upstairs was maintained as a storage facility by the A. A. Kaul Office Supply Company. The

basement was a kind of church. There was a signboard
on the wall above the basement steps, encased in glass.
In neat, movable white block letters on a black field it
read:

LOS ANGELES
HOLINESS PAN-INDIAN RESCUE MISSION
Rev. J. B. B. Tosamah, Pastor & Priest of the Sun
Saturday 8:30 P.M.
"The Gospel According to John"
Sunday 8:30 P.M.
"The Way to Rainy Mountain"
Be kind to a white man today

The basement was cold and dreary, dimly illumi-
nated by two 40-watt bulbs which were screwed into
the side walls above the dais. This platform was made
out of rough planks of various woods and dimensions,
thrown together without so much as a hammer and
nails; it stood seven or eight inches above the floor, and
it supported the tin firebox and the crescent altar. Off to
one side was a kind of lectern, decorated with red and
yellow symbols of the sun and moon. In back of the
dais there was a screen of purple drapery, threadbare
and badly faded. On either side of the aisle which led to
the altar there were chairs and crates, fashioned into
pews. The walls were bare and gray and streaked with
water. The only windows were small, rectangular open-
ings near the ceiling, at ground level; the panes were
covered with a thick film of coal oil and dust, and
spider webs clung to the frames or floated out like
smoke across the room. The air was heavy and stale;
odors of old smoke and incense lingered all around.
The people had filed into the pews and were waiting
silently.

Cruz, a squat, oily man with blue-black hair that
stood out like spines from his head, stepped forward on
the platform and raised his hands as if to ask for the
quiet that already was. Everyone watched him for a
moment; in the dull light his skin shone yellow with

sweat. Turning slightly and extending his arm behind him, he said, "The Right Reverend John Big Bluff Tosamah."

There was a ripple in the dark screen; the drapes parted and the Priest of the Sun appeared, moving shadow-like to the lectern. He was shaggy and awful-looking in the thin, naked light: big, lithe as a cat, narrow-eyed, suggesting in the whole of his look and manner both arrogance and agony. He wore black like a cleric; he had the voice of a great dog:

" *'In principio erat Verbum.'* Think of Genesis. Think of how it was before the world was made. There was nothing, the Bible says. 'And the earth was without form, and void; and darkness was upon the face of the deep.' It was dark, and there was nothing. There were no mountains, no trees, no rocks, no rivers. There was nothing. But there was darkness all around, and in the darkness something happened. *Something happened!* There was a single sound. Far away in the darkness there was a single sound. Nothing made it, but it was there; and there was no one to hear it, but it was there. It was there, and there was nothing else. It rose up in the darkness, little and still, almost nothing in itself—like a single soft breath, like the wind arising; yes, like the whisper of the wind rising slowly and going out into the early morning. But there was no wind. There was only the sound, little and soft. It was almost nothing in itself, the smallest seed of sound—but it took hold of the darkness and there was light; it took hold of the stillness and there was motion forever; it took hold of the silence and there was sound. It was almost nothing in itself, a single sound, a word—a word broken off at the darkest center of the night and let go in the awful void, forever and forever. And it was almost nothing in itself. It scarcely was; but it *was*, and everything began."

Just then a remarkable thing happened. The Priest of the Sun seemed stricken; he let go of his audience and withdrew into himself, into some strange potential of himself. His voice, which had been low and resonant, suddenly became harsh and flat; his shoulders sagged and his stomach protruded, as if he had held his breath to the limit of endurance; for a moment there was a look of amazement, then utter carelessness in his face. Conviction, caricature, callousness: the remainder of his sermon was a going back and forth among these.

"Thank you so much, Brother Cruz. Good evening, blood brothers and sisters, and welcome, welcome. Gracious me, I see lots of new faces out there tonight. *Gracious me!* May the Great Spirit—can we knock off that talking in the back there?—be with you always.

" 'In the beginning was the Word.' I have taken as my text this evening the almighty Word itself. Now get this: 'There was a man sent from God, whose name was John. The same came for a witness, to bear witness of the Light, that all men through him might believe.' Amen, brothers and sisters, *Amen.* And the riddle of the Word, 'In the beginning was the Word. . . .' Now what do you suppose old John *meant* by that? That cat was a preacher, and, well, you know how it is with preachers; he had something big on his mind. Oh my, it was big; it was the *Truth,* and it was heavy, and old John hurried to set it down. And in his hurry he said too much. 'In the beginning was the Word, and the Word was with God, and the Word was God.' It was the Truth, all right, but it was more than the Truth. The Truth was overgrown with fat, and the fat was God. The fat was *John's* God, and God stood between John and the Truth. Old John, see, he got up one morning and caught sight of the Truth. It must have been like a bolt of lightning, and the sight of it made him blind. And for a moment the vision burned on in back of his eyes, and he *knew* what it was. In that instant he saw something he had never seen before and would never see again. That was the instant of revelation, inspiration, Truth. And old John, he must have fallen down on his knees. Man, he must have been shaking and laughing and crying and yelling and praying—all at the same time—and he must have been drunk and delirious with the Truth. You see, he had lived all his life waiting for that one moment, and it came, and it took him by surprise, and it was gone. And he said, 'In the beginning was the Word. . . .' And, man, right then and there he should have stopped. There was nothing more to say, but he went on. He had said all there was to say, everything, but he went on. 'In the beginning was the Word. . . .' Brothers and sisters, *that* was the Truth, the whole of it, the essential and eternal Truth, the bone and blood and muscle of the Truth. But he went on, old John, because he was a preacher. The perfect vision faded from his mind, and he went on. The instant passed, and then he had nothing but a memory. He was desperate and confused, and in his confusion he stumbled and went on. 'In the beginning was the Word, and the Word was with God, and the Word was God.' He went on to talk about Jews and Jerusalem, Levites and Pharisees, Moses and Philip and Andrew and Peter. Don't you see? Old John *had* to go on. That cat had a whole lot at stake. He couldn't let the Truth alone. He couldn't see that he had come to the end of the Truth, and he went on. He tried to make it bigger and better than it was, but instead he only demeaned and encumbered it. He made it soft and big with fat. He was a preacher, and he made a complex sentence of the Truth, two sentences, three, a paragraph. He made a sermon and theology of the Truth. He imposèd his idea of God upon the everlasting Truth. 'In the beginning was the Word. . . .' And that is all there was, and it was enough.

"Now, brothers and sisters, old John was a white man, and the white man has his ways. Oh gracious me, he has his ways. He talks about the Word. He talks through it and around it. He builds upon it with syllables, with prefixes and suffixes, and hyphens and accents. He adds and divides and multiplies the Word. And in all of this he subtracts the Truth. And, brothers and sisters, you have come here to live in the white man's world. Now the white man deals in words, and he deals easily, with grace and sleight of hand. And in his presence, here on his own ground, you are as children, mere babes in the woods. You must not mind, for in this you have a certain advantage. A child can listen and learn. The Word is sacred to a child.

"My grandmother was a storyteller; she knew her way around words. She never learned to read and write, but somehow she knew the good of reading and writing; she had learned how to listen and delight. She had learned that in words and in language, and there only, she could have whole and consummate being. She told stories, and she taught me how to listen. I was a child and I listened. She could neither read nor write, you see, but she taught me how to live among her words, how to listen and delight. 'Storytelling; to utter and to hear . . .' And the simple act of listening is crucial to the concept of language, and more crucial even than reading and writing, and language in turn is crucial to human society. There is proof of that, I think, in all the histories and prehistories of human experience. When that old Kiowa woman told me stories, I listened with only one ear. I was a child, and I took the words for granted. I did not know what all of them meant, but somehow I held on to them; I remembered them, and I remember them now. The stories were old and dear; they meant a great deal to my grandmother. It was not until she died that I knew how *much* they meant to her. I began to think about it, and then I knew. When she told me those old stories, something strange and good and powerful was going on. I was a child, and that old woman was asking me to come directly into the presence of her mind and spirit; she was taking hold of my imagination, giving me to share in the great fortune of her wonder and delight. She was asking me to go with her to the confrontation of something that was sacred and eternal. It was a timeless, *timeless* thing; nothing of her old age or of my childhood came between us.

"Children have a greater sense of the power and beauty of words than have the rest of us in general. And if that is so, it is because there occurs—or reoccurs —in the mind of every child something like a reflection of all human experience. I have heard that the human fetus corresponds in its development, stage by stage, to the scale of evolution. Surely it is no less reasonable to suppose that the waking mind of a child corresponds in the same way to the whole evolution of human thought and perception.

"In the white man's world, language, too—and the way in which the white man thinks of it—has undergone a process of change. The white man takes such things as words and literatures for granted, as indeed he must, for nothing in his world is so commonplace. On every side of him there are words by the millions, an unending succession of pamphlets and papers, letters and books, bills and bulletins, commentaries and conversations. He has diluted and multiplied the Word, and words have begun to close in upon him. He is sated and insensitive; his regard for language—for the Word itself—as an instrument of creation has diminished nearly to the point of no return. It may be that he will perish by the Word.

"But it was not always so with him, and it is not so with you. Consider for a moment that old Kiowa woman, my grandmother, whose use of language was confined to speech. And be assured that her regard for words was always keen in proportion as she depended upon them. You see, for her words were medicine; they were magic and invisible. They came from nothing into sound and meaning. They were beyond price; they could neither be bought nor sold. And she never threw words away.

"My grandmother used to tell me the story of Tai-me, of how Tai-me came to the Kiowas. The Kiowas were a sun dance culture, and Tai-me was their sun dance doll, their most sacred fetish; no medicine was ever more powerful. There is a story about the coming of Tai-me. This is what my grandmother told me:

Long ago there were bad times. The Kiowas were hungry and there was no food. There was a man who heard his children cry from hunger, and he began to search for food. He walked four days and became very weak. On the fourth day he came to a great canyon. Suddenly there was thunder and lightning. A Voice spoke to him and said, "Why are you following me? What do you want?" The man was afraid. The thing standing before him had the feet of a deer, and its body was covered with feathers. The man answered that the Kiowas were hungry. "Take me with you," the Voice said, "and I will give you whatever you want." From that day Tai-me has belonged to the Kiowas.

"Do you see? There, far off in the darkness, something happened. Do you see? Far, far away in the nothingness something happened. There was a voice, a sound, a word—and everything began. The story of the coming of Tai-me has existed for hundreds of years by word of mouth. It represents the oldest and best idea that man has of himself. It represents a very rich literature, which, because it was never written down, was always but one generation from extinction. But for the same reason it was cherished and revered. I could see that reverence in my grandmother's eyes, and I could hear it in her voice. It was that, I think, that old Saint John had in mind when he said, 'In the beginning was the Word. . . .' But he went on. He went on to lay a scheme about the Word. He could find no satisfaction in the simple fact that the Word *was;* he had to account for it, not in terms of that sudden and profound insight, which must have devastated him at once, but in terms of the moment afterward, which was irrelevant and remote; not in terms of his imagination but only in terms of his prejudice.

"Say this: 'In the beginning was the Word. . . .' There was nothing. There was *nothing!* Darkness. There was darkness, and there was no end to it. You look up sometimes in the night and there are stars; you can see all the way to the stars. And you begin to know the universe, how awful and great it is. The stars lie out against the sky and do not fill it. A single star, flickering out in the universe, is enough to fill the mind, but it is nothing in the night sky. The darkness looms around it. The darkness flows among the stars, and beyond them forever. In the beginning that is how it was, but there were no stars. There was only the dark infinity in which nothing was. And something happened. At the distance of a star something happened, and everything began. The Word did not come into being, but *it was*. It did not break upon the silence, but *it was older than the silence and the silence was made of it.*

"Old John caught sight of something terrible. The thing standing before him said, 'Why are you following me? What do you want?' And from that day the Word has belonged to us, who have heard it for what it is, who have lived in fear and awe of it. In the Word was the beginning; *'In the beginning was the Word. . . .'* "

The Priest of the Sun appeared to have spent himself. He stepped back from the lectern and hung his head, smiling. In his mind the earth was spinning and the stars rattled around in the heavens. The sun shone, and the moon. Smiling in a kind of transport, the Priest of the Sun stood silent for a time while the congregation waited to be dismissed.

"Good night," he said, at last, "and get yours."

Why should Abel think of the fishes? He could not understand the sea; it was not of his world. It was an enchanted thing, too, for it lay under the spell of the moon. It bent to the moon, and the moon made a bright, shimmering course upon it, a broad track breaking apart and yet forever whole and infinite, undulating, melting away into furtive islands of light in the great gray, black, and silver sea. "Beautyway," "Bright Path," "Path of Pollen"—his friend Benally talked of these things. But Ben could not have been thinking of the moonlit sea. No, not the sea, not this. The sea . . . and small silversided fishes spawned mindlessly in correlation to the phase of the moon and the rise and fall of the tides. The thought of it made him sad, filled him with sad, unnamable longing and wonder.

It was cold. It was dark and cold and damp, and he could not open his eyes. He was in pain. He had fallen down; that was it. He was lying face down on the ground, and it was cold and there was a roaring of the sea in his brain and there was a fog rolling in from the sea. The pain was very great, and his body throbbed with it; his mind rattled and shook, wobbling now out of a spin, and he could not place the center of the pain. And he could not see. He could not open his eyes to see. Something was wrong, terribly wrong. When he awoke, he tried to move; he was numb with cold, but the effort to move brought new pain, sharp, then massive pain. It was so great that he fainted, and the next time he knew better than to move suddenly. The effect of the alcohol was wearing off. In another moment he began to retch, his whole body contracting, quaking involuntarily, and again the pain mounted and his mind was slipping away. He wanted to die. An hour passed in which he lay still and mindless in the cold. Beyond the steady crashing of the sea there were sounds of the city at night, ticking on like a clock toward the dawn. He could hear foghorns away in the distance, and he did not know what they were. Out in the immense gray silence of the sea, ships were steaming in from the Orient.

After a while he could open one of his eyes a little, enough to see. He was lying in a shallow depression in which there were weeds and small white stones and tufts of long gray grass. There was a fence on the bank before him; at his back there was a broad rocky beach, tilting to the sea. The fence was made of heavy wire mesh, and on the other side there were tractors and trailers, the long line of a roof. There were trademarks and lines of letters on the trailers—and on some of the cabs as well—but he could not make out the words. The yard was dark except for a single light on the wall of the warehouse, above the loading dock; but the light was across the yard, and it was dim and fuzzy in the fog. There were cans and bits of paper and broken glass against the fence; he was close to the fence; he could

almost touch it. He raised himself to reach for the fence
and the pain struck him again. He slumped, his body
stiffening and folding over the pain, as if to crush it
out. But the pain was too great, and the contraction
only made it worse. Gradually he relaxed, and the pain
ran to his hands. It concentrated there. His hands were
broken, and he could not move them. Some of his
fingers were stuck together with blood, and the blood
was dry and black. The sight of his hands made him
sick. His mind boggled and withdrew . . . and it came
around again to the fishes.

He had loved his body. It had been hard and quick
and beautiful; it had been useful, quickly and surely
responsive to his mind and will. He was thick in the
chest and shoulders, not so powerful as his grandfather,
but longer of reach and more agile. And his hands were
slender and strong. His legs were lean and tapered,
long-muscled, too thin for a white man's legs: the legs of
an Indian. Once he could have run all day, really run,
not jogging but moving fast over distances, without
ruining his feet or burning himself out. He had never
been sick until he was sick with alcohol. The disease
which killed his mother and Vidal never even touched
him, as far as he knew. But once he had fallen from a
horse, and for days afterward there was a sharp, recurrent pain in the small of his back. Francisco chanted
and prayed; the old man applied herbs and powders
and potions and salves, and nothing worked. And at
last Abel went to fat Josie. She was getting on in years
by then—and he was almost a grown man—but she
picked him up from behind as if he were a sack full of
straw and drew him close against her so that he was
sitting on the great hump of her belly, and her mighty
arms tightened under his ribs until he could not
breathe. And then she shook him—not much, gently—
until he was loose in his arms and legs. She put him
down with a wink and a grunt, and he was all right
again. Fat Josie. His body was mangled and racked
with pain. His body, like his mind, had turned on him;
it was his enemy.

Angela put her white hands to his body.
Abel put his hands to her white body.

Forever is the sea. Away in the fog there was a
crashing of the sea. He thought of the trial, six years
before. After six years he could remember the white
man's body, how it lay limp and lifeless in the night
rain, bright like phosphorus almost; the angle of the
body and its limb; the white shining hand, open and
obscene. But he could remember very little about the
trial. There were charges, questions, and answers; it
was ceremonial, orderly, civilized, and it had almost
nothing to do with him.

"I mean," said Father Olguin, "that in his own mind
it was not a man he killed. It was something else."
"An evil spirit."
"Something like that, yes."
"Can you be more precise, Father?"
The priest wanted to affect great humility and say,
"Ah no, my son," but instead he said: "We are dealing
with a psychology about which we know very little. I
see the manifestations of it every day, but I have no
real sense of it—not any longer. I relinquished *my*
claim to the psychology of witchcraft when I left home
and became a priest. Anyway, there is no way to be
objective or precise about such a thing. What shall I
say? I believe that this man was moved to do what he
did by an act of imagination so compelling as to be
inconceivable to us."
"Yes, yes, yes. But *these* are the facts: he killed a
man—took the life of another human being. He did so
of his own volition—he has admitted that—he was
armed for no other reason. He committed a brutal and
premeditated act which we have no choice but to call
by its right name."
"Homicide is a legal term, but the law is not my
context; and certainly it isn't his—"
"*Murder* is a moral term. *Death* is a universal human
term."

When he had told his story once, simply, Abel re-
fused to speak. He sat like a rock in his chair, and after
a while no one expected or even wanted him to speak.
That was good, for he should not have known what
more to say. Word by word by word these men were
disposing of him in language, *their* language, and they
were making a bad job of it. They were strangely
uneasy, full of hesitation, reluctance. He wanted to help
them. He could understand, however imperfectly, what
they were doing to him, but he could not understand
what they were doing to each other. When it was
finished, he took the hand which was held out to him.
There was such pain in the priest's eyes that he could
not bear to look into them. He was embarrassed, hu-
miliated; he hated the priest for suffering so.

He had killed the white man. It was not a compli-
cated thing, after all; it was very simple. It was the
most natural thing in the world. Surely they could see
that, these men who meant to dispose of him in words.
They must know that he would kill the white man
again, if he had the chance, that there could be no
hesitation whatsoever. For he would know what the
white man was, and he would kill him if he could. A
man kills such an enemy if he can.

He awoke coughing; there was blood in his throat
and mouth. He was shuddering with cold and pain. He
had been moaning softly until he choked; now he was
gasping for breath. There was a faint vibration under
him. *Be quiet!* He had to be quiet; something was going
on. He peered into the night: all around the black land
against the star-bright, moon-bright sky. So far had his
vision reached that the owl, when he saw it, seemed to
fly in his face and break apart, torrential, ghostly, silent
as a dream. He was delirious now and gasping for
breath; he hurried on in his mind, holding the owl
away in the corner of his eye. The owl watched him
without meaning, and something was going on. There
was the faintest tremor at his feet. The night was infinite and serene, and there was an owl in the darkness

and a tremor in the earth. He got down on his knees
and put his ear to the ground. Men were running
toward him. He left the road and hid away in the
brush, and soon he could see them in the distance, the
old men running after evil, their white leggings holding
in motion like smoke above the ground. They passed in
the night, full of tranquillity, certitude. There was no
sound of breathing or sign of effort about them. They
ran as water runs.

There was a burning at his eyes.

The runners after evil ran as water runs, deep in the
channel, in the way of least resistance, no resistance.
His skin crawled with excitement; he was overcome
with longing and loneliness, for suddenly he saw the
crucial sense in their going, of old men in white leggings running after evil in the night. They were whole
and indispensable in what they did; everything in
creation referred to them. Because of them, perspective,
proportion, design in the universe. Meaning because of
them. They ran with great dignity and calm, not in the
hope of anything, but hopelessly; neither in fear nor
hatred nor despair of evil, but simply in recognition
and with respect. Evil was. Evil was abroad in the
night; they must venture out to the confrontation; they
must reckon dues and divide the world.

Now, here, the world was open at his back. He had
lost his place. He had been long ago at the center, had
known where he was, had lost his way, had wandered
to the end of the earth, was even now reeling on the
edge of the void. The sea reached and leaned, licked
after him and withdrew, falling off forever in the abyss.
And the fishes . . .

        Age and date of birth:
        Sex:
        Height:
        Weight:
        Color hair:
        Color eyes:
        Married:

Children (ages):
Religious affiliation (optional):
Education (circle appropriate completed years of
    schooling):
Father's name (age and occupation if living):
Mother's name (age and occupation if living):

The walls of his cell were white, or perhaps they
were gray or green; he could not remember. After a
while he could not imagine anything beyond the walls
except the yard outside, the lavatory and the dining
hall—or even the walls, really. They were abstractions
beyond the reach of his understanding, not in themselves confinement but symbols of confinement. The
essential character of the walls consisted not in their
substance but in their appearance, the bare one-
dimensional surface that was white, perhaps, or gray, or
green.

Do you prefer the company of men or of women?
Do you drink alcoholic beverages to excess often, oc-
    casionally, not at all?
Which would you prefer to watch, a tennis match or a
    bullfight?
Do you consider yourself of superior, above average,
    average, below average intelligence?

He tried to think where the trouble had begun, what
the trouble was. There was trouble; he could admit that
to himself, but he had no real insight into his own
situation. Maybe, certainly, *that* was the trouble; but he
had no way of knowing. He wanted a drink; he wanted
to be drunk. The bus leaned and creaked; he felt the
surge of motion and the violent shudder of the whole
machine on the gravel road. The motion and the sound
seized upon him. Then suddenly he was overcome with
a desperate loneliness, and he wanted to cry out. He
looked toward the fields, but a low rise of the land lay
before them. The town had settled away into the earth.
There was a curve and the bus pitched and swung. It
made him giddy, and he wanted to laugh. He was

wearing a pair of brown-and-white shoes which fat
Josie had given to him. They had belonged to a man
for whom fat Josie's daughter had worked as a house-
keeper in the city. The man died and his widow gave
away his clothes. The shoes were beautiful, almost new,
thin-soled, sharply pointed, with angles and whorls of
perforation. There were metal taps on the heels, and the
leather creaked. They were too large for Abel, but he
wore them anyway, had waited a long time for the
occasion to wear them. And now and then in the bus he
looked at them, would slide the instep and toe of one
and then the other along the backs of his legs to remove
the dust and bring out the shine, would flex the soles to
hear them squeak.

But the shoes were brown and white. They were
new, almost, and shiny and beautiful; and they
squeaked when he walked. In the only frame of refer-
ence he had ever known, they called attention to themselves, simply, honestly. They were brown and white;
they were finely crafted and therefore admirable in the
way that the work of a good potter or painter or
silversmith is admirable: the object is beautiful in itself,
worthy of appreciation as a whole and for its own
sake. But now and beyond his former frame of refer-
ence, the shoes called attention to Abel. They were
brown and white; they were conspicuously new and too
large; they shone; they clattered and creaked. And they
were nailed to his feet. There were enemies all around,
and he knew that he was ridiculous in their eyes.

Please complete each of the following in one or two
words. (It is important that you complete this section as
quickly as possible, filling in each of the blanks with the
first response that comes to mind.)

I would like ————.
I am not ————.
Rich people are ————.
I am afraid of ————.
It is important that I ————.
I believe strongly in ————.

The thing I remember most clearly is ———.
As a child I enjoyed ———.
Someday I shall ———.
People who laugh loudly are ———.

etc.

Milly?

"No test is completely valid," she said. "Some are more valid than others."

But Milly believed in tests, questions and answers, words on paper. She was a lot like Ben. She believed in Honor, Industry, the Second Chance, the Brotherhood of Man, the American Dream, and him—Abel; she believed in him. After a while he began to suspect as much, and . . .

That night—he could not remember how it came about; he had got a little drunk—he made love to her. He had been watching her. She was always coming around when he and Ben were at home. There was no shyness in her. She had looked him squarely in the eye, had spoken up and laughed—she was always laughing—from the very first. Easy laughter was wrong in a woman, dangerous and wrong. She was plain in the face; her eyes were too small and her mouth too large. But she had yellow hair and her body was supple and ripe. He had watched her, how she walked away, her feet close together and her steps swinging not from the knees but from the hips, slowly, easily; and her hips were full and rolling. She had big breasts.

She was talking to him and laughing, and her laughter was real and ringing. But he was sullen. He was not listening to her but wanting her, thinking of how to have her. And she knew what he was thinking, and her voice and laughter grew sudden and a little too thin and she began to play with her hands. It was a long time since she had given herself to a man. She had nearly forgotten what to think about, worry about, dwell upon. And it was all right: she was big and plain and breathing hard, but she felt small and beautiful and dear among her things. The flat where she lived was

dingy and cheaply done, but she said to herself that it
was charming and quaint and tastefully arranged. Her
bedroom was colorless and cluttered with brassy trin-
kets and smelled of stale and sour air, but, no, she said,
there was a kind of warmth and character to it, milk
glass and marble and brownish photographs in antique
oval frames; there was a fragrance of clean, fresh linen
and lilac water. They were sitting on the side of her
bed.

He drew her to him carefully and placed his mouth
very lightly on her arm. His hand rose along her arm,
and her arm grew taut. She had stopped talking. She
was responsive and soft and yielding in his arms. He
kissed her and stroked her hair. He unfastened her
dress and laid it open and drew it down from her
shoulders; her shoulders were round and freckled and
smooth. He unhooked her brassiere and it fell away
from her breasts, which were white and brown-tipped
and good-smelling. He fondled one of her breasts. Her
mouth was open and working slowly under his own,
like a small animal, and she arched her back and thrust
her breasts out to him. He kissed her mouth and her
eyes and her hair and her throat and her shoulders. She
closed her eyes and lay back, still and seemingly relaxed, save that her skin sprang to his touch, until he
kissed her nipples. He held one of her breasts with the
tips of his fingers, so lightly and carefully that it might
have been a bead of rain, and sucked it for a long time.
She moaned a little, cradling his head, and her legs
stirred against him. In another moment she turned on
her side and drew her dress and her half slip and her
panties down over one hip, and he slid his hand down
from her breast and along the slope of her side. She was
wide in the hips and the twist of her body so, with her
shoulders forward and her breasts outthrust against him,
accentuated the curve and width of her hips, and they
were smooth and round and white. He moved his hand
slowly to the top of the curve of her hip, over, and
down her buttocks. She set her feet on the floor and
arched her body so that her buttocks closed together

and were tight and he worked her clothing down to her ankles and she got free of it. He kissed her on the mouth again and returned his hand to the full white lumps of her buttocks, which were relaxed and loose and heavy now, and glazed with sweat, to the deep cleavage between the long dark tufts of hair, damp and fine and crinkled. And her own hands were gentle, touched him gently. He waited, keening to her, but her excitement never made her wild. At the height of her desire he held her away for an instant; she was open-mouthed and moaning. Her eyes rolled under their lids and her whole body trembled, and her body was full and white and glowing and glistening. His nostrils flared to the odor of her body, and he was brutal with her.

The sea crashed and roared. There was a slow, terrible burning at his eyes, and he could not move his hands. His whole body was breaking open to the roar of the sea.

Tosamah, orator, physician, Priest of the Sun, son of Hummingbird, spoke:

" 'Peyote is a small, spineless, carrot-shapted cactus growing in the Rio Grande Valley and southward. It contains nine narcotic alkaloids of the isoquinoline series, some of them strychnine-like in physiological action, the rest morphine-like. Physiologically, the salient characteristic of peyote is its production of visual hallucinations or color visions, as well as kinesthetic, olfactory, and auditory derangements.' Or, to put it another way, that little old woolly booger turns you on like a light, man. Daddy peyote is the vegetal representation of the sun."

The Priest of the Sun was going to conduct a prayer meeting, and he had painted himself for it. The part in his hair was a bright yellow line; there were vertical red lines on either side of his face; and there were yellow half moons under his eyes. He was a holy, sinister sight. Everything was ready. He stepped upon the platform with a gourd rattle and staff in one hand and the paraphernalia satchel in the other. One by one the celebrants followed and sat down in a circle. Cristóbal Cruz was the fireman, Napoleon Kills-in-the-Timber the drummer.

The fire blazed in a pan at the center of the circle. The Priest of the Sun sat west of the fire, between the fireman and the drummer. Before him was the low earthen altar in the shape of a crescent, horns to the east. It rose from either end to the center, where there was a small flat space, a kind of cradle for the father peyote. There was a fine groove which ran the length of the altar; the groove symbolized the life of man from birth, ascending from the southern tip to the crest of power and wisdom at the center, and thence in descent through old age to death at the northern tip. When everyone was seated in place, the Priest of the Sun laid a bunch of sage sprigs on the altar, and there he placed the fetish.

The drum was a potbellied, cast-iron, three-legged No. 6 trade kettle with the bail ears filed off, half filled with water in which live coals and herbs were dropped. The buckskin head was made taut, and the sound of the drum was mellow and low like distant thunder. The Priest of the Sun spread a clean white cloth before him on the floor, and on this he placed the things which he removed from the paraphernalia satchel:

1. A fine fan of fancy pheasant feathers.
2. A slender beaded drumstick.
3. A packet of brown cigarette papers.
4. A bundle of sage sprigs.
5. A smokestick bearing the sacred water-bird symbol.
6. A pouch of powdered cedar incense.
7. An eagle-bone whistle.
8. A paper bag containing forty-four peyote buttons.

The first ceremony was begun. The Priest of the Sun made a cigarette out of Bull Durham and brown paper, then passed the makings to his left. When everyone had made a cigarette, Cruz took up a burning stick and handed it to Tosamah. The Priest of the Sun lit his cigarette and passed the stick to his left. When all were smoking, he prayed, saying, "Be with us tonight." Then he held his cigarette out to the fetish, that it also might smoke. Others prayed.

The incense-blessing ceremony followed. The Priest of the Sun sprinkled dry rubbed cedar on the fire, then made four circular motions toward the flames, holding in his hand the bag of peyote buttons. Having done this, he removed four of the buttons and passed the remainder to his left. Kneeling, he bruised a tuft of sage between his palms, inhaling deeply of the scent, and rubbed his hands on his head and chest, shoulders and arms and thighs. The others imitated him, first holding out their hands to receive the blessing of the incense, then rubbing themselves.

Then all the celebrants ate of the peyote buttons, spitting out the woolly centers. From then on until dawn there were songs, prayers, the sound of the rattle and the drum. The fire leaped upward from the pan in a single flame, and the flame wavered and danced. Everyone was looking at it, and after a while there was a terrible restlessness, a sheer wave of exhilaration in the room. There was no center to it; it was everywhere at once. Everyone felt himself young and whole and powerful. No one was sick or weak or weary. Everyone wanted to run and jump and laugh and breathe deeply of the air. Everyone wanted to shout that he was hale and playful and everlastingly alive, but no one said anything; they waited. And directly the fire stood still, and everyone grew sad. There was a great falling down of the spirit, and everyone rocked back and forth in misery and despair. The flames gave off wisps of black smoke, and an awful sense of grief rose up in the room. Everyone thought of death, and the thought was overwhelming in itself. Everyone was caught up in the throes of a deadly depression. There was general nausea, and the dullest pain of the mind. And slowly, slowly the flame hardened and grew bright. It receded to a point at the depth of vision; there was a pale aura all about it, and in this there began to radiate splinters of light, white and red and yellow. And the process of radiation quickened and grew. At last there was nothing in the world but a single point of light, brilliant, radiant to infinity; and from it there arose in the radiance wave upon wave of purest color, rose and red and scarlet and carmine and wine. And to these was added a sudden burst of yellow: butter and rust and gold and saffron. And final fire—the one essence of all fires from the beginning of time, there in the most beautiful brilliant bead of light. And flares of blue and green emerged from the bead and burst, and it was not the blue and green of turquoise and emeralds, or of water and grass, but far more intensely beautiful than these, crystalline and infused with the glare and glitter of the sun. And there was sound. The gourd danced in Tosamah's hand, and there was a rushing and rolling of rain on the roof, a rockslide rumbling, roaring. And beneath and beyond, transcendent, was the drum. The drumbeats gathered in the room and the flame quivered to the beat of the drum and thunder rolled in the somewhere hills. The sound was building, building. The first and last beats of the drum were together in the room and the gulf between was growing tight with sound and the sound was terrible and deep, shivering like the pale, essential flame. And then the sound did not diminish but backed away to the walls, and everyone waited. And at the center of the circle, rising and holding over the fetish and the flame, there were voices, one after another:

Henry Yellowbull:
    "Be with us tonight. Come to us now in bright colors and sweet smoke. Help us to make our way. Give us laughter and good feelings always. Listen, I want to honor you with my prayer. I want to give something, these words. Listen."

Cristóbal Cruz:
    "Well, I jes' want to say thanks to all my good frens here tonight for givin' me this here honor, to be fire-

man an' all. This here shore is a good meetin', huh? I
know we all been seein' them good visions an' all, an'
there's a whole lot of frenhood an' good will aroun'
here, huh? I jes' want to pray out loud for prosper'ty
an' worl' peace an' brotherly love. In Jesus' name.
Amen."

Napoleon Kills-in-the-Timber:

"Great Spirit be with us. We gone crazy for you to be
with us poor Indi'ns. We been bad long time 'go, just
raise it hell an' kill each others all the time. An' that's
why you 'bandon us, turn you back on us. Now we pray
to you for help. Help us! We been suffer like hell some
time now. Long, long time 'go we throw it in the towel.
Gee whiz, we want be frens with white mans. Now I
talk to you, Great Spirit. Come back to us! Hear me
what I'm say tonight. I am sad because we die. The ol'
people they gone now . . . oh, oh. They tol' us to do it
this way, sing an' smoke an' pray. . . . [Here Kills-in-
the-Timber began to wail, and his body quaked with
weeping. No one was ashamed, and after a time he regained possession of himself and went on.] Our chil-
drens are need your help pretty damn bad, Great Spirit.
They don' have no respec' no more, you know? They
are become lazy, no-good-for-nothing drunkerts. Thank
you."

Ben Benally:

"Look! Look! There are blue and purple horses . . . a
house made of dawn. . . ."

At midnight there was a lull in the sound and
motion of the world. The fire was going out, and the
circle of men swayed in and out very slowly to the
small, pulsating flame. And from every angle of vision,
there at the point of the flame was the fetish; it seemed
to swell and contract in the silence, and the odor of
sage became so heavy in the room that it burned in the
nostrils. The Priest of the Sun arose and went out. Far
off a juke box began to fill one corner of the night with
brassy music, and there were occasional sounds of
traffic in the streets. Then in the agony of stasis they

heard it, one shrill, piercing note and then another, and another, and another: four blasts of the eagle-bone whistle. In the four directions did the Priest of the Sun, standing painted in the street, serve notice that something holy was going on in the universe.

Abei's face was cut and broken, and there was a burning at his eyes, a terrible irritation at the corners of his eyes, and he wanted to bring his hands to them. The pain jarred him wide awake. One of his eyes opened a little, and through the slit he could see his hands; they were twisted and mangled, the thumbs splayed back and broken at the joints. He could remember that each of his thumbs had been slowly, almost gently twisted inward to the palms until the bone above the first knuckle was screwed tight into the joint and at last the ball of the bone was sprung from the socket with a loud popping sound. His hands were black with blood and huge with swelling, like rubber gloves. The fog thickened about him until he could no longer see even his hands. He had the sense that his whole body was shaking violently, tossing and whipping, flopping like a fish. Then he realized that beyond the pain of his broken body he was cold, colder than he had ever been before. He tried to cry out, but only a hoarse rattle and wheezing came from his throat.

Sometimes he would go to fat Josie after his mother died, and fat Josie would speak kindly to him or give him sweet things to eat. And when no one else was there she would make faces and carry on like an idiot, trying to make him laugh. He was a child who did not laugh, and fat Josie had no children of her own, only the daughter who was grown and lived away in the city. Francisco clicked his tongue and said that his grandsons ought to be left alone, but fat Josie just lifted her leg and broke wind, sneering the old man away. And the children huddled against her and laid their heads on her great brown arms. And the week after Vidal was buried, Abel went to her for the last time as a child, and Francisco never knew. She crossed her eyes and stuck out her tongue and danced around the kitchen on her huge bare feet, snorting and breaking wind like a horse. She carried her enormous breasts in her hands, and they spilled over and bobbed and swung about like water bags, and her great haunches quivered and heaved, straining against her ancient, greasy dress, and her broad shining face cracked in a wonderfully stupid, four-teeth-missing grin, and all the while tears were streaming from her eyes.

Milly?

He was afraid. He heard the sea breaking, saw shadowy shapes in the swirling fog, and he was afraid. He had always been afraid. Forever at the margin of his mind there was something to be afraid of, something to fear. He did not know what it was, but it was always there, real, imminent, unimaginable.

"He was not afraid, no, sir," Bowker said. Abel was listening to him, self-conscious, growing angry and confused that this white man should talk about him, account for him, as if he were not there.

"Mitch—I mean Corporal Rate—and me were dug in on the side of thirteen, and we could see south along the ridge. The shelling had stopped a little while before and Corporal Rate and Private Marshall and me were the only ones to get out—except for *him*, I mean—and, hell, we didn't even know he was still alive. He must have been knocked out. Well, sir, Marshall, he got ahead of Mitch and me. He went on over the top of thirteen, and Mitch—Corporal Rate—and me dug in when we heard the tank coming up. We could see both sides of the ridge, sir. That tank was just zigzagging up to the ridge slow and easy, just cleaning up, sir. Reconnaissance. I had the glasses on it. Well, I was studying that mother pretty hard, and pretty soon Mitch, he punched me and pointed down the hill. It was him, sir, the chief, and he was moving around. He had raised up and was looking at the ridge, looking for that tank, sir.

Jesus, that's the first we knew of him being alive. Everybody else was dead, see, and that tank was just cleaning up, making sure. Anyway, he was just coming to, I guess, and that tank was at the ridge. Jesus, sir. Well, he put his head down at the last minute and played dead. We didn't know if they had seen him or not, and, Jesus, that tank hitched over and it was coming right down on him, it looked like. But they *hadn't* seen him, and it went on by, about as close as it could without running over him. *Jesus!* Mitch— Corporal Rate—he swore and I was holding my breath. And that's when the chief here got up, sir. Oh Jesus, he just all of a sudden got up and started jumping around and *yelling* at that goddam tank, and it was maybe thirty, forty yards is all down the hill. Oh Jesus, sir. He was giving it the finger and whooping it up and doing a goddam *war dance,* sir. Me and Mitch, we just groaned. We couldn't *believe* what was going on. And there *he* was, hopping around with his finger up in the air and giving it to that tank in Sioux or Algonquin or something, for crissake. And he didn't have no weapon or helmet even. And, sir, that goddam tank all of a sudden crunched down and bounced— yes, sir, *bounced,* actually bounced to a stop—and they all started shooting at him, *pop, pop, ping, ping, pow!* Jesus, we could see the leaves kicking up all around him, and him whooping it up like a—like a—I don't know what, sir. Yes, sir, clapping whoops from his mouth just like in the movies—and all the time that finger was up theirs, sir. Then finally he took off through the trees kind of crazy and casual like, *dancing!* He would kind of dodge around, then let out a whoop and do a goddam two-step or something and light out again, giving it to them behind and under- hand, and them goddam bullets going *pop, pop, ping, ping, pow*. Oh Jesus, sir. *Jesus!*"

Milly?
Oh God, his hands hurt.
There was a black hole in the fog, and for a moment

the light above the loading dock receded and became a point, sharp and minute and far away; and then the swirling fog closed over it again and it drew close like the moon and began to throb.

And they were getting close to the river, and a cloud drew across the face of the moon and the center of the cloud was lead gray and full of dark patches like smoke and they also moved across the moon, and the edge of the cloud was silver and sharp and billowing even as it moved across the throbbing November moon. And other, elongated clouds hung out against the sky, the near ones moving like drift on the water, and the dunes were glowing faintly, almost vibrating with low light. He crept along behind his brother, bending low and weaving after him through the brush-covered dunes, going silently on the cold ripples of sand. And Vidal took smaller, higher steps as they approached the water and held the gleaming shotgun ready, perfectly balanced and slightly away from his body. Downriver, in an angle of the black land, Abel could see the moonlight glistening on the broad curve of the river and hear beyond the rise of the dunes the lapping of the water. Then Vidal, without looking around, motioned for him to be still; he crouched and waited. They were at the base of a long drift, the opposite side of which sloped gently down to the riverbank. Vidal got down on his stomach and crawled on his elbows and knees to the top of the drift. He motioned again, and Abel followed. From the top of the drift they could see a good stretch of the river; at the far reaches it gleamed and glittered like crumpled foil, but directly below it was black and invisible, for there was a long thicket of willows and tamarack on the opposite bank. There were narrows upstream, where the river branched around a bar of rocks and reeds. And just beyond, where the streams converged, there was the faintest quiver on the moonlit water, a dance of lights against the black hills in the distance. Then Abel held his breath. The gleam of metal caught his eye, and he saw Vidal taking aim into

the darkness. He flinched in anticipation of the shot
and searched the river below. He could see nothing at
first. But even before the gun roared, the black water
shattered and crawled. The gray geese, twenty-four of
them, broke from the river, lowly, steadily on the rise
of sound, straining to take hold on the air. Their effort
was so great that they seemed for a time to hang
beating in the willows, helplessly huge and frantic. But
one after another they rose southward on their great
thrashing wings, trailing bright beads of water in their
wake. Then they were away, and he had seen how they
craned their long slender necks to the moon, ascending
slowly into the far reaches of the winter night. They
made a dark angle on the sky, acute, perfect; and for
one moment they lay out like an omen on the bright
fringe of a cloud.

*Did you see? Oh, they were beautiful! Oh Vidal, oh
my brother, did you see?*

An awful stillness returned on the water, and without looking away Vidal pointed. Abel could barely see
it then, the dark shape floating away in the blackness.
And when he waded after it, the current was slow and
steady and there was no sound on the river. The bird
held still in the cold black water, watching him. He was
afraid, but the bird made no move, no sound. He took
it up in his hands and it was heavy and warm and the
feathers about its keel were hot and sticky with blood.
He carried it out into the moonlight, and its bright
black eyes, in which no terror was, were wide of him,
wide of the river and the land, level and hard upon the
ring of the moon in the southern sky.

Milly?

The moon and the water bird.

Milly?

What, honey? What is it?

*Oh Milly oh God the pain my hands my hands are
broken.*

He tried to open the other eye, both eyes wide, but
he could not. He stared into the blackness that pressed
upon and within him. The backs of his eyelids were

black and murky like the fog; microscopic shapes, motes and bits of living thread floated obliquely down, were buoyed up again, and vanished in the great gulf of his blindness. He did not know how to tell of his pain; it was beyond his power to name and assimilate.

Oh Milly the water birds were beautiful I wish you could have seen them I wanted my brother to see them they were flying high and far away in the night sky and there was a full white moon and a ring around the moon and the clouds were long and bright and moving fast and my brother was alive and the water birds were so far away in the south and I wanted him to see them they were beautiful and please I said please did you see them how they pointed with their heads to the moon and flew through the ring of the moon. . . .

"Milly?"

"Yes, honey."

"Did you like it, Milly? It was good again, wasn't it, Milly?"

"Oh honey, I liked it."

"I'm going out tomorrow, Milly. I'm going to look for a job."

"You bet. You'll find a good job if you keep looking. Sometimes it's hard."

"I'm going to find one tomorrow, Milly. You'll see."

"I know it, honey."

"Listen, I'm going to get a good job, and Saturday or Sunday you and me and Ben, let's go to the beach, O.K.?"

"Oh yes, I hope so."

"It was good again, Milly."

"It was lovely. I love you."

They made love in the afternoons when she came home early from work. Sometimes he wasn't there when she came in, and she knew that he was drunk again, sick, in trouble maybe. Then she kept still and waited for the night, and when it came she listened to music or ironed clothes or went to the movies. And afterward she undressed and got into bed and lay very still in the dark, listening. And at such times she was

very lonely and afraid, and she wanted to cry. But she
did not cry.

*And somewhere beyond the cold and the fog and the
pain there was the black and infinite sea, bending to the
moon, and there was the cold white track of the moon
on the water. And far out in the night where nothing
else was, the fishes lay out in the black waters, holding
still against all the force and motion of the sea; or close
to the surface, darting and rolling and spinning like
lures, they played in the track of the moon. And far
away inland there were great gray migrant geese riding
under the moon.*

She had been in Los Angeles four years, and in all
that time she had not talked to anyone. There were
people all around; she knew them, worked with them—
sometimes they would not leave her alone—but she did
not talk to them, tell them anything that mattered in the
least. She greeted them and joked with them and
wished them well, and then she withdrew and lived her
life. No one knew what she thought or felt or who she
was.

And one day he was there by her door, waiting for
her. It was a hot, humid afternoon and the streets were
full of people when she walked home. And he was
waiting for her. They had not known each other very
long, and he was still full of shyness. He was waiting
for her, glad just to see her, and she knew it. He was
saying something, trying to tell her why he had come;
and suddenly she realized how lonely they both were,
how unspeakably lonely. She began to shake her head
and bite her lip, and the tears rolled down her cheeks
and she made no sound except that now and then she
had to catch her breath, crying as an old person cries.
And through her tears she saw all his confusion and
alarm, how pitifully funny he was, and she had to let
go of all the sobbing laughter that was in her—and
later on, when their desire was spent, a little of the
pain.

*I was a dirty child with yellow hair and thin little
arms and legs that were big at the joints. I didn't wear*

shoes, and the soles of my feet were hard and cracked and black with dirt. I could run like a rabbit. Once, when Daddy was fencing off a lot behind the barn, I ran into a strand of barbed wire and cut myself deep across the chest. Here, give your hand. These are the scars, almost invisible now—the skin is shinier and a little lighter in color, that's all—and if you lift or squeeze me there so that the skin is relaxed, tiny ridges form in the scars. There are little blue and purple veins beneath the scars, blue mostly. Isn't it funny how the veins go here and there, back and forth, all over, all over?

The earth where we lived was hard and dry and brick-red, and Daddy plowed and planted and watered the land, but in the end there was only a little yield. And it was the same year after year after year; it was always the same, and at last Daddy began to hate the land, began to think of it as some kind of enemy, his own very personal and deadly enemy. I remember he came in from the fields at evening, having been beaten by the land, and he said nothing. He never said anything; he just sat down and thought about his enemy. And sometimes his eyes grew wide and his mouth fell open in disbelief, as if all at once he knew, knew that he had tried everything and failed, and there was nothing left to do but sit there in wonder of his enemy's strength. And every day before dawn he went to the fields without hope, and I watched him, sometimes saw him at sunrise, far away in the empty land, very small on the skyline, turning to stone even as he moved up and down the rows.

Daddy loved me; it wasn't anything that he could put into words or deeds beyond the simple act of turning each day against the land, but I knew it. It was a deep, desperate kind of love; there was no laughter to it at all. "Listen," he said, "you've got to get away," and his eyes were almost wild with the thought of it. He gave me the money that he had been saving against that moment for seventeen years, and together we walked to Fletcher's farm, and Daley Fletcher drove us

*to the railroad in his father's truck. The train came and
Daddy handed me the suitcase, and when I took it I
touched his big, scarred, sunburned hand, and it was
hard and gnarled like a root and good to smell like
deep, dark earth that has just been turned, and I said,
"Bye, Daddy—Daddy, goodbye."*

*And I never saw him again, and I remember still
how he looked at the railroad station in his overalls and
striped coat and the shiny black shoes that I saw him
wear only two or three times in all those years. And
after a while the money he had given to me was gone,
but I was big and strong and I knew how to work and I
worked as a waitress after school and got up before
daylight to read and study. And in my last year at
school I fell in love with Matt and married Matt. We
were happy and nothing bad happened to us for a
while. We had a baby; she was soft and beautiful and
we named her Carrie. And when Matt went away and
did not come back, I gave all of my love to Carrie; it
was all right because of her, because of Carrie. I found
a job and someone to stay with Carrie, and on week-
ends I played with Carrie and sang Carrie to sleep and
in the afternoons if the weather was good I took Carrie
to the playground and pushed her in the swing and
Carrie held on tight with her little hands and laughed
and laughed, Carrie laughed.*

*And Carrie was four. She was crying and I went into
her room and she was burning up with fever, and in the
night she had gone sallow and pale and weak. Her
voice was strange and thin, and there were dark circles
under her eyes. She seemed very small and delicate and
beautiful. I went downstairs and called the doctor from
the drugstore on the corner. And as I was leaving, Mr.
Hitchcock spoke to me—hello, I guess, or can I help
you—and I looked at him and his mouth fell open and
I saw all my fear and helplessness in his face. And for
no reason at all he laughed; the sound of it seemed to
horrify him.*

*The doctor came and took Carrie away in an ambu-
lance. She seemed to know what was happening to her,*

and at the hospital she lay very still, looking at the ceiling. She seemed not afraid but curious, strangely thoughtful and wise. To me that was the most unreasonable, terrifying thing of all: that my child should be so calm in the face of death. She seemed to come of age, to live out a whole lifetime in those few hours, and at last there was a look of infinite wisdom and old age on her little face. And sometime in the night she asked me if she was going to die. And do you see how it was? There was no time for deceit, and I didn't even have the right to look away. "Yes," I said. And she asked me what it was like to die, and I answered, "I don't know." "I love you, Milly," she said; she had never called me by my name before. In a little while she looked very hard at the ceiling, and her eyes blazed for a moment. Then she turned her head a little and closed her eyes. She seemed very tired. "I love you so much," she whispered, and she did not wake up again.

He had to get up. He would die of exposure unless he got up. His legs were all right; at least his legs were not broken. He brought one of his knees forward, then the other, and he managed to get to the fence. He struggled for a long time, and at last he was sitting up with his back to the fence. Upright, his mind cleared, and for the time being there was no longer any danger of fainting. He gathered his feet under him and braced himself against the fence; by pressing first the back of his head and then his shoulders to the fence, using his legs to force himself upward and backward, he stood up. Then he began a long and tortuous journey through dark alleys and streets. Sometimes cars passed through the streets, and he waited in the shadows for them to go by and flattened himself against the walls of buildings. At some point along the way there was a truck, a three-quarter-ton pickup with a covered bed, open at the back. The lights were on. He leaned over the open tailgate and rolled himself inside. In a while someone came and got into the cab; the truck pulled away and Abel gave himself up to pain and exhaustion. And later the truck stopped and he got out and went on again

through the shadows and along the walls. Once a man
came around a corner and saw him. The man's mouth
opened as if to say something, and for a moment he
stopped and stared; then he walked away, hurriedly,
out of sight.

Now and then Abel stopped to rest, and a dizziness
came over him and he had to go on. His mind was
buckling with fatigue. He thought of the fog, stumbled
and rolled his shoulders on the wet brick walls in the
swirling fog, and in his pain and weariness he saw
Milly and Ben running on the beach and he was there
on the beach with Milly and Ben and the moon was
high and bright and the fishes were far away in the
depths and there was nothing but the moonlight and the
long white margin of the sea on the beach.

JANUARY 27

Tosamah, orator, physician, Priest of the Sun, son of Hummingbird, spoke:

"A single knoll rises out of the plain in Oklahoma, north and west of the Wichita range. For my people it is an old landmark, and they gave it the name Rainy Mountain. There, in the south of the continental trough, is the hardest weather in the world. In winter there are blizzards which come down the Williston corridor, bearing hail and sleet. Hot tornadic winds arise in the spring, and in summer the prairie is an anvil's edge. The grass turns brittle and brown, and it cracks beneath your feet. There are green belts along the rivers and creeks, linear groves of hickory and pecan, willow and witch hazel. At a distance in July or August the steaming foliage seems almost to writhe in fire. Great green and yellow grasshoppers are everywhere in the tall grass, popping up like corn to sting the flesh, and tortoises crawl about on the red earth, going nowhere in the plenty of time. Loneliness is there as an aspect of the land. All things in the plain are isolate; there is no confusion of objects in the eye, but *one* hill or *one* tree or *one* man. At the slightest elevation you can see to the end of the world. To look upon that landscape in the early morning, with the sun at your back, is to lose the sense of proportion. Your imagination comes to life, and this, you think, is where Creation was begun.

"I returned to Rainy Mountain in July. My grandmother had died in the spring, and I wanted to be at her grave. She had lived to be very old and at last infirm. Her only living daughter was with her when she

117

died, and I was told that in death her face was that of a child.

"I like to think of her as a child. When she was born, the Kiowas were living the last great moment of their history. For more than a hundred years they had controlled the open range from the Smoky Hill River to the Red, from the headwaters of the Canadian to the fork of the Arkansas and Cimarron. In alliance with the Comanches, they had ruled the whole of the Southern Plains. War was their sacred business, and they were the finest horsemen the world has ever known. But warfare for the Kiowas was pre-eminently a matter of disposition rather than survival, and they never understood the grim, unrelenting advance of the U.S. Cavalry. When at last, divided and ill-provisioned, they were driven onto the Staked Plain in the cold of autumn, they fell into panic. In Palo Duro Canyon they abandoned their crucial stores to pillage and had nothing then but their lives. In order to save themselves, they surrendered to the soldiers at Fort Sill and were imprisoned in the old stone corral that now stands as a military museum. My grandmother was spared the humiliation of those high gray walls by eight or ten years, but she must have known from birth the affliction of defeat, the dark brooding of old warriors.

"Her name was Aho, and she belonged to the last culture to evolve in North America. Her forebears came down from the high north country nearly three centuries ago. The earliest evidence of their existence places them close to the source of the Yellowstone River in western Montana. They were a mountain people, a mysterious tribe of hunters whose language has never been classified in any major group. In the late seventeenth century they began a long migration to the south and east. It was a journey toward the dawn, and it led to a golden age. Along the way the Kiowas were befriended by the Crows, who gave them the culture and religion of the plains. They acquired horses, and their ancient nomadic spirit was suddenly free of the ground. They acquired Tai-me, the sacred sun dance doll, from that moment the chief object and symbol of their worship, and so shared in the divinity of the sun. Not least, they acquired the sense of destiny, therefore courage and pride. When they entered upon the Southern Plains, they had been transformed. No longer were they slaves to the simple necessity of survival; they were a lordly and dangerous society of fighters and thieves, hunters and priests of the sun. According to their origin myth, they entered the world through a hollow log. From one point of view, their migration was the fruit of an old prophecy, for indeed they emerged from a sunless world.

"I could see that. I followed their ancient way to my grandmother's grave. Though she lived out her long life in the shadow of Rainy Mountain, the immense landscape of the continental interior—all of its seasons and its sounds—lay like memory in her blood. She could tell of the Crows, whom she had never seen, and of the Black Hills, where she had never been. I wanted to see in reality what she had seen more perfectly in the mind's eye.

"I began my pilgrimage on the course of the Yellowstone. There, it seemed to me, was the top of the world, a region of deep lakes and dark timber, canyons and waterfalls. But, beautiful as it is, one might have the sense of confinement there. The skyline in all directions is close at hand, the high wall of the woods and deep cleavages of shade. There is a perfect freedom in the mountains, but it belongs to the eagle and the elk, the badger and the bear. The Kiowas reckoned their stature by the distance they could see, and they were bent and blind in the wilderness.

"Descending eastward, the highland meadows are a stairway to the plain. In July the inland slope of the Rockies is luxuriant with flax and buckwheat, stonecrop and larkspur. The earth unfolds and the limit of the land recedes. Clusters of trees, and animals grazing far in the distance, cause the vision to reach away and wonder to build upon the mind. The sun follows a longer course in the day, and the sky is immense be-

yond all comparison. The great billowing clouds that
sail upon it are shadows that move upon the grass and
grain like water, dividing light. Farther down, in the
land of the Crows and the Blackfeet, the plain is yellow.
Sweet clover takes hold of the hills and bends upon
itself to cover and seal the soil. There the Kiowas
paused on their way; they had come to the place where
they must change their lives. The sun is at home on the
plains. Precisely there does it have the certain character
of a god. When the Kiowas came to the land of the
Crows, they could see the dark lees of the hills at dawn
across the Bighorn River, the profusion of light on the
grain shelves, the oldest deity ranging after the solstices. Not yet would they veer south to the caldron of
the land that lay below; they must wean their blood
from the northern winter and hold the mountains a
while longer in their view. They bore Tai-me in procession to the east.

"A dark mist lay over the Black Hills, and the land
was like iron. At the top of a ridge I caught sight of
Devils Tower—the uppermost extremity of it, like a
file's end on the gray sky—and then it fell away behind
the land. I was a long time then in coming upon it, and
I did not see it again until I saw it whole, suddenly
there across the valley, as if in the birth of time the core
of the earth had broken through its crust and the
motion of the world was begun. It stands in motion,
like certain timeless trees that aspire too much into the
sky, and imposes an illusion on the land. There are
things in nature which engender an awful quiet in the
heart of man; Devils Tower is one of them. Man must
account for it. He must never fail to explain such a
thing to himself, or else he is estranged forever from the
universe. Two centuries ago, because they could not do
otherwise, the Kiowas made a legend at the base of the
rock. My grandmother said:

Eight children were there at play, seven sisters and their
brother. Suddenly the boy was struck dumb; he trembled
and began to run upon his hands and feet. His fingers be-

came claws, and his body was covered with fur. There was a bear where the boy had been. The sisters were terrified; they ran, and the bear after them. They came to the stump of a great tree, and the tree spoke to them. It bade them climb upon it, and as they did so it began to rise into the air. The bear came to kill them, but they were just beyond its reach. It reared against the tree and scored the bark all around with its claws. The seven sisters were borne into the sky, and they became the stars of the Big Dipper.

"From that moment, and so long as the legend lives, the Kiowas have kinsmen in the night sky. Whatever they were in the mountains, they could be no more. However tenuous their well-being, however much they had suffered and would suffer again, they had found a way out of the wilderness.

"The first man among them to stand on the edge of the Great Plains saw farther over land than he had ever seen before. There is something about the heart of the continent that resides always in the end of vision, some essence of the sun and wind. That man knew the possible quest. There was nothing to prevent his going out; he could enter upon the land and be alive, could bear at once the great hot weight of its silence. In a sense the question of survival had never been more imminent, for no land is more the measure of human strength. But neither had wonder been more accessible to the mind nor destiny to the will.

"My grandmother had a reverence for the sun, a certain holy regard which now is all but gone out of mankind. There was a wariness in her, and an ancient awe. She was a Christian in her later years, but she had come a long way about, and she never forgot her birthright. As a child, she had been to the sun dances; she had taken part in that annual rite, and by it she had learned the restoration of her people in the presence of Tai-me. She was about seven years old when the last Kiowa sun dance was held in 1887 on the Washita River above Rainy Mountain Creek. The buffalo were gone. In order to consummate the ancient sacrifice—to impale the head of a buffalo bull upon the Tai-me tree—a delegation of old men journeyed into Texas, there to beg and barter for an animal from the Goodnight herd. She was ten when the Kiowas came together for the last time as a living sun dance culture. They could find no buffalo; they had to hang an old hide from the sacred tree. That summer was known to my grandmother as Ä'poto Etódä-de K'ádó, Sun Dance When the Forked Poles Were Left Standing, and it is entered in the Kiowa calendars as the figure of a tree standing outside the unfinished framework of a medicine lodge. Before the dance could begin, a company of armed soldiers rode out from Fort Sill under orders to disperse the tribe. Forbidden without cause the essential act of their faith, having seen the wild herds slaughtered and left to rot upon the ground, the Kiowas backed away forever from the tree. That was July 20, 1890, at the great bend of the Washita. My grandmother was there. Without bitterness, and for as long as she lived, she bore a vision of deicide.

"Now that I can have her only in memory, I see my grandmother in the several postures that were peculiar to her: standing at the wood stove on a winter morning and turning meat in a great iron skillet; sitting at the south window, bent above her beadwork, and afterward, when her vision failed, looking down for a long time into the fold of her hands; going out upon a cane, very slowly as she did when the weight of age came upon her; praying. I remember her most often at prayer. She made long, rambling prayers out of suffering and hope, having seen many things. I was never sure that I had the right to hear, so exclusive were they of all mere custom and company. The last time I saw her, she prayed standing by the side of her bed at night, naked to the waist, the light of a kerosene lamp moving upon her dark skin. Her long black hair, always drawn and braided in the day, lay upon her shoulders and against her breasts like a shawl. I did not always understand her prayers; I believe they were made of an older language than that of ordinary speech. There was something inherently sad in the sound, some slight hesitation upon the syllables of sorrow. She began in a high and descending pitch, exhausting her breath to silence; then again and again—and always the same intensity of effort, of something that is, and is not, like urgency in the human voice. Transported so in the dim and dancing light among the shadows of her room, she seemed beyond the reach of time, as if age could not lay hold of her. But that was illusion; I think I knew then that I should not see her again.

"Houses are like sentinels in the plain, old keepers of the weather watch. There, in a very little while, wood takes on the appearance of great age. All colors soon wear away in the wind and rain, and then the wood is burned gray and the grain appears and the nails turn red with rust. The windowpanes are black and opaque; you imagine there is nothing within, and indeed there are many ghosts, bones given up to the land. They stand here and there against the sky, and you approach them for a longer time than you expect. They belong in the distance; it is their domain.

"My grandmother lived in a house near the place where Rainy Mountain Creek runs into the Washita River. Once there was a lot of sound in the house, a lot of coming and going, feasting and talk. The summers there were full of excitement and reunion. The Kiowas are a summer people; they abide the cold and keep to themselves, but when the season turns and the land becomes warm and vital they cannot hold still; an old love of going returns upon them. The old people have a fine sense of pageantry and a wonderful notion of decorum. The aged visitors who came to my grandmother's house when I was a child were men of immense character, full of wisdom and disdain. They dealt in a kind of infallible quiet and gave but one face away; it was enough. They were made of lean and leather, and they bore themselves upright. They wore great black hats and bright ample shirts that shook in the wind. They rubbed fat upon their hair and wound their braids with strips of colored cloth. Some of them painted their faces and carried the scars of old and cherished enmities. They were an old council of war lords, come to remind and be reminded of who they were. Their wives and daughters served them well. The women might indulge themselves; gossip was at once the mark and compensation of their servitude. They made loud and elaborate talk among themselves, full of jest and gesture, fright and false alarm. They went abroad in fringed and flowered shawls, bright beadwork and German silver. They were at home in the kitchen, and they prepared meals that were banquets.

"There were frequent prayer meetings, and great nocturnal feasts. When I was a child, I played with my cousins outside, where the lamplight fell upon the ground and the singing of the old people rose up around us and carried away into the darkness. There were a lot of good things to eat, a lot of laughter and surprise. And afterward, when the quiet returned, I lay down with my grandmother and could hear the frogs away by the river and feel the motion of the air.

"Now there is a funeral silence in the rooms, the endless wake of some final word. The walls have closed in upon my grandmother's house. When I returned to it in mourning, I saw for the first time in my life how small it was. It was late at night, and there was a white moon, nearly full. I sat for a long time on the stone steps by the kitchen door. From there I could see out across the land; I could see the long row of trees by the creek, the low light upon the rolling plains, and the stars of the Big Dipper. Once I looked at the moon and caught sight of a strange thing. A cricket had perched upon the handrail, only a few inches away from me. My line of vision was such that the creature filled the moon like a fossil. It had gone there, I thought, to live and die, for there of all places was its small definition made whole and eternal. A warm wind rose up and purled like the longing within me.

"The next morning I awoke at dawn and went out of my grandmother's house to the scaffold of the well that stands near the arbor. There was a stillness all around, and night lay still upon the pecan groves away by the river. The sun rose out of the ground, powerless for a long time to burn the air away, dim and nearly cold like the moon. The orange arc grew upon the land, curving out and downward to an impossible diameter. It must not go on, I thought, and I began to be afraid; then the air dissolved and the sun backed away. But for a moment I had seen to the center of the world's being. Every day in the plains proceeds from that strange eclipse.

"I went out on the dirt road to Rainy Mountain. It was already hot, and the grasshoppers began to fill the air. Still, it was early in the morning, and birds sang out of the shadows. The long yellow grass on the mountain shone in the bright light, and a scissortail hied above the land. There, where it ought to be, at the end of a long and legendary way, was my grandmother's grave. She had at last succeeded to that holy ground. Here and there on the dark stones were the dear ancestral names. Looking back once, I saw the mountain and came away."

3

THE
NIGHT CHANTER

Los Angeles, 1952

FEBRUARY 20

He left today. It was raining, and I gave him my
coat. You know, I hated to give it up; it was the only
one I had. We stood outside on the platform. He was
looking down, and I was trying to think of something
to say. The tracks were all wet—you know how the
rails shine in the rain—and there were people all
around, saying goodbye to each other. He had a sack
and a suitcase—you know, one of those little tin boxes
with three stripes painted on it. We had walked all the
way in the rain, and the shoulders of that coat—his
coat—were all wet and stained. He tried to keep the
sack inside of his coat, but part of it got wet. He took it
out and tried to dry it when we got to the station, but it
was already getting soft. I guess it fell apart afterward.
He looked pretty bad. His hands were still bandaged,

and he couldn't use them very well. It took us a long time to get there. He couldn't walk very fast. It was a good coat, gray gabardine, but it was old and it hadn't been cleaned in a long time. I don't remember where I got it. I got it secondhand, and there was a big hole in the right pocket. You don't really need a coat like that around here, except when it rains.

It was getting dark when I came back, and it stopped raining for a while. I got downtown and the streets were wet and all the lights were going on. You know, it's dark down there all the time, even at noon, and the lights are always on. But at night when it rains the lights are everywhere. They shine on the pavement and the cars. They are all different colors; they go on and off and move all around. The stores are all lighted up inside, and the windows are full of shiny things. Everything is clean and bright and new-looking.

You have to watch where you're going. There's always a big crowd of people down there, especially after it rains, and a lot of noise. You hear the cars on the wet streets, starting and stopping. You hear a lot of whistles and horns, and there's a lot of loud music all around. Those old men who stand around on the corners and sell papers, they're always yelling at you, but you can't understand them. I can't, anyway.

I walked right along because it was going to rain again, and I was getting cold. I didn't want to be down there anyway. I kept thinking about him being sick like that on the train. He looked pretty bad, like he might need some help. There was still a lot of blue and swelling around his eyes, and you could see that his nose was broken. His hands were all bandaged up. Now you know you're not going to help a man who's all beat up like that, not if you don't know him. You're going to be afraid of him. I kept thinking about that, how nobody was going to help him, and I got to feeling bad; I got lonesome, too, I guess. It started to rain again, and it was kind of lonesome down there in the streets, everybody going someplace, going home.

I came out of the tunnel on 3rd Street and turned

around toward Bunker Hill Avenue. It was raining pretty hard again, and my shirt was all wet and sticky—you know how wool smells when it gets all wet—and I went into The Silver Dollar, Henry's place. It was warm in there. It's a pretty good place; there's a juke box, and there's always some Indians, drinking and fooling around. You can get drunk in there, and as long as you don't get sick or start a fight or something, nobody says anything. Martinez comes in there sometimes, and then everybody gets real quiet. You know, they call him *culebra*. He's a cop, and a bad one. He's always looking for trouble, and if he's got it in for you—if you make him mad—you better look out. But Henry always gives him a bottle—and money, too, I guess. He's good to him, you know? And if you behave yourself in there, he lets you alone.

It was pretty crowded on account of the rain. I wanted a drink, but I didn't have any money, so I asked Manygoats if he could pay me back. He was with some girl I didn't know—she's new around here, from Oklahoma, I think—and he's owed me some money for a long time. He gets paid by the week, and he gets some lease money from home, too. He was acting pretty big, because of that girl, I guess, and he gave me three dollars. She was good-looking, that girl—you know, great big breasts—and I kind of wanted to meet her. I could have talked to her, I guess; she seemed real nice and friendly, but I could tell that Manygoats wanted me to leave. He was making out all right; he had some plans, I guess. So I told him I had to meet somebody outside, and he sure was glad. If he hadn't paid me back, I could have had some fun with him. Right away I was sorry I said that—about meeting somebody, I mean—because then I had to leave. There were some other guys I knew, Howard and Tosamah and Cruz and those guys, but they were all having a big time together. They had some plans, I guess. I guess I didn't care much, either. I didn't feel like going anyplace, so I bought a bottle of wine and came on home.

You could see the rain around the streetlights. They

made funny yellow circles against the clouds and the buildings, and the rain was steady and fine. It was dark out there, except for the streetlights, and there was nobody around, just a car now and then. And it would go along pretty slow and sound like it does in the rain, and when it passed you could see the tail-lights, how they make those wavy red lines in the street.

There's no light downstairs; it blew out a long time ago. There was nobody around. I couldn't hear anybody, and the stairs were dark. I forgot to get some matches at Henry's place, and I had to feel my way up the stairs. When I came in here, the window was open. That's the first thing I saw, that the window was open and the rain was coming in and the sill was dripping inside. I felt bad about that, forgetting to close the window, because the floor leaks and that old woman Carlozini downstairs, she gets pretty mad. It leaks on her bed, I guess, and one time she told the landlord about it. I turned on the light and, sure enough, there was a big wet spot on the floor. I tried to wipe it up, but it was pretty well soaked in. She's out someplace again, and I hope she really ties one on. She's going to tell the landlord as sure as anything. Well, it's the only window in here, you know, and it gets pretty stale if you don't keep it open. You have to open the door, too, so there's a draft. I remember how I was sitting there this afternoon with my feet up on the sill. It was just beginning to sprinkle a little, and he had that little suitcase out on the bed, and I could hear him moving around behind me. There was a big pigeon flying around out there in the street, and I was trying to get it to come up on the sill. You know, you can do that sometimes if you put some crumbs around. But that one—it was a great big one, with a lot of blue and purple on its neck—it couldn't seem to make up its mind. It just sailed around for a while, and finally it flew up on the roof across the street. There were some others over there, a lot of them. We just forgot about that window, that's all.

It was pretty cold in here when I came in, and I took

off that wet shirt and turned the radiator on. I was afraid the furnace wasn't on, but pretty soon the pipes began knocking and there was a little heat coming out. I put my shirt over the radiator, and pretty soon you could really smell the wool. It got almost dry, and I was afraid it was going to get burned, so I put it on again. It was all warm, and it really felt good. I thought about eating something. Milly brought some groceries up here yesterday; she's always doing that, and it comes out of her own pocket, too. We put some cheese and crackers and a couple of candy bars in that sack he had. There's quite a bit left, I guess, some bread and some cans of chili and stuff. But I wasn't very hungry, and I had that bottle of wine. Now that he's gone, I don't know if Milly's going to come around anymore. I guess she will. It got pretty hot in here after a while, and I had to turn the heat off. It's funny how those pipes make all that noise. You can hear them all over the building, especially when there's nobody around.

I kept thinking about him. I wish Milly was here. She liked him a whole lot, and she's always talking to me about him. She thought he was going to be O.K. around here, I guess. She wouldn't get drunk with us or anything like that, but she would always come around with some groceries and we would eat together, the three of us. She was always asking him about the reservation and the army and prison and all at first, but he didn't like to talk about it much, and she caught on after a while. And then she talked about other things. We kidded her a lot, and she liked it, and pretty soon she didn't bring all those papers around anymore. She was new on the job, and at first she used to bring a lot of questionnaires and read them to us, a lot of silly questions about education and health and the kind of work we were doing and all, and she would write down a lot of that stuff. I didn't care, but he got mad about it and said it wasn't any of her business. She took it all right, and that's when she stopped bringing all those forms and things around. He started to like her after that, and I was glad. We got along pretty well together.

She was sorry to see him go. She wouldn't let on, but I could tell that she felt pretty bad. She had to work today, or I guess she would have gone down to the station with us. Maybe she'll come around tomorrow. Maybe not.

I kept thinking about last night, too. We went up there on the hill, him and me, with Tosamah and Cruz. There were a lot of Indians up there, and we really got going after a while. We were all pretty drunk by that time, and there were a couple of drums, and some guy had a flute. There was a lot of liquor up there, and everybody was feeling pretty good. We started singing some of those real old-time songs, and it was still and cool up there. Somebody built a fire, and we heated the drums until they were good and tight and you could really hear them. And pretty soon they started to dance. Mercedes Tenorio had some turtle shells and she started a stomp dance. You know, she was going all around with those shells in the firelight and calling out just like an old-timer, "Ee he! Oh ho! Ah ha!" And everybody started to answer in the same way, and they all got behind her and she was leading them all around. I kind of wanted to get in there, too, but he didn't care much about it, and he couldn't dance anyway on account of being all banged up like that, so we just stood back and watched.

You can forget about everything up there. We could see all the lights down below, a million lights, I guess, and all the cars moving around, so small and slow and far away. We could see one whole side of the city, all the way to the water, but we couldn't hear anything down there. All we could hear was the drums and the singing. There were some stars, and it was like we were way out in the desert someplace and there was a squaw dance or a sing going on, and everybody was getting good and drunk and happy.

He wanted to tell me something, and we went off a little way by ourselves. We were both pretty drunk, and we just stood around out there in the dark, listening. I guess we were thinking the same thing. I don't know

what he wanted to say. I guess he wanted *me* to say
something first, so I started to talk about the way it was
going to be. We had some plans about that. We were
going to meet someplace, maybe in a year or two,
maybe more. He was going home, and he was going to
be all right again. And someday I was going home, too,
and we were going to meet someplace out there on the
reservation and get drunk together. It was going to be
the last time, and it was something we had to do. We
were going out into the hills on horses and alone. It was
going to be early in the morning, and we were going to
see the sun coming up. It was going to be good again,
you know? We were going to get drunk for the last
time, and we were going to sing the old songs. We were
going to sing about the way it used to be, how there
was nothing all around but the hills and the sunrise and
the clouds. We were going to be drunk and, you know,
peaceful—beautiful. We had to do it a certain way, just
right, because it was going to be the last time.

I told him about that. It was a plan we had. You
know, I made all of that up when he was in the
hospital, and it was just talk at first. But he believed in
it, I guess, and the next day he asked me about it. I had
to remember what it was, and then I guess I started to
believe in it, too. It was a plan we had, just the two of
us, and we weren't ever going to tell anybody about it.

"House made of dawn." I used to tell him about
those old ways, the stories and the sings, Beautyway
and Night Chant. I sang some of those things, and I
told him what they meant, what I thought they were
about. We would get drunk, both of us, and then he
would want me to sing like that. Well, we were up there
on the hill last night, and we could hear the drums and
the flute away off, and it was dark and cool and peaceful. I told him about the plan we had, and we were
getting pretty drunk, and I started to sing all by myself.
The others were singing, too, but it was the wrong kind
of thing, and I wanted to pray. I didn't want them to
hear me, because they were having a good time, and I

was ashamed, I guess. I kept it down because I didn't
want anybody but him to hear.

> *Tségihi.*
> House made of dawn,
> House made of evening light,
> House made of dark cloud,
> House made of male rain,
> House made of dark mist,
> House made of female rain,
> House made of pollen,
> House made of grasshoppers,
> Dark cloud is at the door.
> The trail out of it is dark cloud.
> The zigzag lightning stands high upon it.
> Male deity!
> Your offering I make.
> I have prepared a smoke for you.
> Restore my feet for me,
> Restore my legs for me,
> Restore my body for me,
> Restore my mind for me,
> Restore my voice for me.
> This very day take out your spell for me.
> Your spell remove for me.
> You have taken it away for me;
> Far off it has gone.
> Happily I recover.
> Happily my interior becomes cool.
> Happily I go forth.
> My interior feeling cool, may I walk.
> No longer sore, may I walk.
> Impervious to pain, may I walk.
> With lively feelings, may I walk.
> As it used to be long ago, may I walk.
> Happily may I walk.
> Happily, with abundant dark clouds, may I walk.
> Happily, with abundant showers, may I walk.
> Happily, with abundant plants, may I walk.
> Happily, on a trail of pollen, may I walk.
> Happily may I walk.
> Being as it used to be long ago, may I walk.
> May it be beautiful before me,

May it be beautiful behind me,
May it be beautiful below me,
May it be beautiful above me,
May it be beautiful all around me.
In beauty it is finished.

He was unlucky. You could see that right away. You could see that he wasn't going to get along around here. Milly thought he was going to be all right, I guess, but she didn't understand how it was with him. He was a longhair, like Tosamah said. You know, you have to change. That's the only way you can live in a place like this. You have to forget about the way it was, how you grew up and all. Sometimes it's hard, but you have to do it. Well, he didn't want to change, I guess, or he didn't know how. He came here from prison, too, and that was bad. He was on parole, and he had to do everything right the first time. That made it a lot harder for him; he wasn't as lucky as the rest of us. He was going to get us all in trouble, Tosamah said. Tosamah sized him up right away, and he warned me about him. But, you know, Tosamah doesn't understand either. He talks pretty big all the time, and he's educated, but he doesn't understand.

One night I was up here by myself—he was out someplace—and Tosamah came in. I didn't much want to talk to him, you know, because he's always showing off and making fun of things. He was feeling pretty good, I guess, and he started right in the way he does. "You take that poor cat," he said. "They gave him every advantage. They gave him a pair of shoes and told him to go to school. They deloused him and gave him a lot of free haircuts and let him fight on their side. But was he grateful? Hell, no, man. He was too damn dumb to be civilized. So what happened? They let him alone at last. They thought he was harmless. They thought he was going to plant some beans, man, and live off the fat of the land. Oh, he was going to make his way, all right. He would get some fat little squaw all knocked up, and they would lie around all

day and get drunk and raise a lot of little government
wards. They would make some pottery, man, and boost
the economy. But it didn't turn out that way. He turned
out to be a real primitive sonuvabitch, and the first
time he got hold of a knife he killed a man. That must
have embarrassed the hell out of them.

"And do you know what he said? I mean, do you
have any *idea* what that cat said? A *snake,* he said. He
killed a goddam *snake! The corpus delicti,* see, *he
threatened to turn himself into a snake,* for crissake,
and rattle around a little bit. Now ain't that something,
though? Can you *imagine* what went on at that trial?
There was this longhair, see, cold sober, of sound
mind, and the goddam judge looking on, and the prose-
cutor trying to talk sense to that poor degenerate Indian:
'Tell us about it, man. Give it to us straight.' 'Well, you
honors, it was this way, see? I cut me up a little snake
meat out there in the sand.' Christ, man, that must have
been our finest hour, better than Little Bighorn. That
little no-count cat must have had the whole Jesus
scheme right in the palm of his hand. Think of it!
What's-His-Name v. United States. I mean, where's the
legal precedent man? When you stop to think about it,
due process is a hell of remedy for snakebite.

"They put that cat away, man. They *had* to. It's part
of the Jesus scheme. *They,* man. They put all of us
renegades, us diehards, away sooner or later. They've
got the right idea. They put us away before we're born.
They're an almighty wise and cautious bunch, those
cats, full of discretion. You've got to admire them,
man; they know the score. I mean they see through us.
They know what we're waiting for. We don't fool them
for a minute. Listen here, Benally, one of these nights
there's going to be a full red moon, a hunter's moon,
and we're going to find us a wagon train full of women
and children. Now you won't believe this, but I drink
to that now and then."

He's always going on like that, Tosamah, talking
crazy and showing off, but he doesn't understand. I got
to thinking about it, though, anyway. About *him;*

about him being afraid of that man out there, so afraid
he didn't know what to do. That, you know, being so
scared of something like that—that's what Tosamah
doesn't understand. He's educated, and he doesn't believe in being scared like that. But he doesn't come
from the reservation. He doesn't know how it is when
you grow up out there someplace. You grow up out
there, you know, someplace like Kayenta or Luka-
chukai. You grow up in the night, and there are a
lot of funny things going on, things you don't know
how to talk about. A baby dies, or a good horse. You
get sick, or the corn dries up for no good reason. Then
you remember something that happened the week before, something that wasn't right. You heard an owl,
maybe, or you saw a funny kind of whirlwind; somebody looked at you sideways and a moment too long.
And then you *know*. You just know. Maybe your aunt
or your grandmother was a witch. Maybe you knew she
was, because she was always going around at night,
around the corrals; maybe you saw her sometimes, like
she was talking to the dogs or the sheep, and when you
looked again she wasn't there. You just know, and you
can't help being scared. It was like that with him, I
guess. It might have been like that.

We got along all right; we had some pretty good
times. I remember the first time he came around. It was
pretty early. I had been there about an hour, I guess,
and the foreman called me. I thought he was going to
bawl me out because I had punched in late, but I guess
he didn't know about that. I went into the office, and
there *he* was, with the foreman and some other guy, a
Relocation officer. We shook hands and the foreman
said he was going to start him out on my line, and
would I show him around? I was glad, because De-
Benedictus had been laid off the week before, and there
was nobody across from me on the line and I didn't
have anybody to talk to. I needed a stapler pretty bad,
too, because I was having to do two jobs and a lot of
orders were piling up. Well, I showed him how to
punch in and took him around to meet some of the

guys. I could tell he was kind of shy and scared—you know how it is when you start to work in a new place—and then I took him over to my line and showed him how to staple. He was good with his hands, and he caught on all right. He was just learning, you know, and it was kind of slow at first. He made some mistakes, too, but I played like I didn't notice, and after a while we were turning those things out pretty good.

He was looking right down at his work all the time, like I wasn't even there. I knew how he felt, so I didn't try to talk to him, and every time it slowed up we just stood there looking up the line for the next piece, like we were really busy thinking about it, you know, and it was part of the job. It was getting on toward noon, and I noticed that he hadn't brought a lunch bag. I was trying to think what I ought to do about that. I didn't know if he had any money. It's funny, but I hadn't thought about that before, and I got to worrying about it. I didn't want to embarrass him or anything, and I guess he was thinking about it, too, because when the whistle blew he acted like he didn't know what it was and went right on working. Anyway, it turned out all right. We punched out, and I took him over to the Coke machine. He had some Relocation money, I guess. He had some change, anyway, and I was glad. We got a couple of Cokes and went on out into the yard. Everybody was sitting around out there eating lunch. They were being pretty friendly, too, but I didn't want to get in with them because I knew he would have been embarrassed. They kid around a lot down there, those guys. They're always calling you chief and talking about firewater and everything. I don't mind, but I didn't know how he would take it. I was afraid it might hurt his feelings or something. He was used to it, though, because he had been in the army, and in prison, too, but I didn't know that then. Right away we went off by ourselves. I had a sandwich, and I asked him if he wanted to split it with me, but he said he wasn't hungry. I ate about half of it and acted like I didn't want any more. I put the rest of it down on the plank between us and kept hoping he would change his mind and take it, but he didn't. Finally I had to throw it away.

He didn't have anyplace to stay. The Relocation people were looking around, I guess, but they hadn't found a place, and he was going to spend the night at the Indian Center. There's a storeroom down there in the alley, where they keep the food and clothing that people have donated, you know. You can stay there sometimes if you don't have anyplace else to go. It's just an old frame building, and you can see through the cracks in the walls, but you can make a pretty good bed out of those old coats and things, and you can keep warm. But there's no toilet and no lights, and somebody's always bringing a girl in there to fool around. A lot of guys get sick in there, too, and it always smells kind of sour and bad. I told him about that and said he could move in with me if he wanted to. He didn't say anything, but after work he went down and talked to the Relocation people, and that night he came with that little suitcase up to my room.

It was a long time before he would talk to anyone. Oh, after a while we talked a whole lot, him and me, but it was about things that happened around here. You know, Milly and those other social workers would come around sometimes, and we kidded around about them afterward. We got in with some of the other guys and got drunk and fooled around. But it was a long time before he would talk about himself—and then he never said much. I guess it's that way with most of us. If you come from the reservation, you don't talk about it much; I don't know why. I guess you figure that it won't do you much good, so you just forget about it. You think about it sometimes; you can't help it, but then you just try to put it out of your mind. There's a whole lot more to think about, and it mixes you up sometimes if you don't just go along with it. I guess if we all came from the same place it would be different;

we could talk about it, you know, and we could understand.

We were kind of alike, though, him and me. After a while he told me where he was from, and right away I knew we were going to be friends. We're related somehow, I think. The Navajos have a clan they call by the name of that place. I was there once, too. That was eight or ten years ago, I guess, and I was going to the Santa Fe Indian School, and some of us went over there for the big dance they have in November. It was cold that winter, and there was a lot of snow all around. It's a pretty good place; there are mountains and canyons around there, and there's a lot of red in the rocks. Except for the mountains, it's like the land south of Wide Ruins, where I come from, full of gullies and brush and red rocks. And he didn't have any family, either, just his grandfather. He said his grandfather used to have a bunch of sheep. I herded sheep from the time I could walk.

It didn't snow much out there, but when it did the whole land as far as you could see was covered with it. It went on sometimes all night, and you could see it outside through the smoke hole, swirling around in the black sky. And sometimes the flakes came in and melted on the floor around the fire, and you were glad there was a fire. You could hear the wind, and you were little and you could get way down under the blankets and see the firelight moving around on the logs of the roof and the walls, and the floor was yellow and warm and you could put your hand in the dust and feel how warm it was. And you knew that your grandfather was there, looking out for you. You woke up sometimes, and he was there stirring the fire to keep it going, and you knew that everything was all right. And the next morning you got up and went out and it was cold and there was snow all around. Maybe the sun was out and the snow was so bright it hurt your eyes. It drifted up against the hogan and covered the top of it, and the hogan looked like a little hill all covered with snow and

you could see the smoke coming out of it and smell the
coffee and the mutton. You put your hands in the snow
and rubbed your face with it and it made you come
alive and feel good and your hands were red and wet
with the cold snow. You were little and you looked all
around at the snow; it was piled up on the brush and
you could see the dark branches under it, and the sheep
were bleating in the corral and the poles of the fence
were heaped high with snow, and underneath you
could see the wood, how it was almost black with
water. There was a gully a little way off, and inside of
it, where the snow had fallen off, the earth was a deep
red and there were bits of brush growing out of it and
covered with snow. They looked like handfuls of cotton
or wool. Everything was changed. It was bright and
beautiful all around, and you felt like yelling and running and jumping up and down. You went in and put
your hands to the fire. Your grandfather scolded you
and smiled, because you were little and he knew how
you felt. He cut off a piece of mutton and put it down
for you. You could smell the coffee and hear it boiling
in the pot, even after he took it off the fire and poured
it into the cups. You could see it, how black and hot it
was, and there was a lot of smoke coming out of the
cups. You had to let it set a while because the cups
were made of enamelware and they could burn your
hands. It was hard to wait, because you were cold and
you knew how good it was going to taste. But the meat
cooled right away and you could pick it up and it made
your fingers warm. The fat was full of juice and smoke,
and sometimes there was a little burned crust on it,
hard black flakes that you could feel on your teeth,
and the meat was tough and good to chew. And after a
while you could pick up the cup and hold it in your
hands. It was good just to hold it. You could see the
dull shine of it, where the grease from your fingers was,
and the black smoking coffee inside. And when you
drank it, it was better than the meat. You could feel it
all good and hot and strong inside of you, and the good
hard grounds on your teeth and tongue. You hurried,

*because you were little and the snow was outside and
there was a lot to do. You took the sheep out in the
bright morning and had to look for grass under the
snow. It was hard to find and you had to brush the
snow off of it and your hands were wet and ached with
cold. But you were happy anyway, because you were
out with the sheep and could talk and sing to yourself
and the snow was new and deep and beautiful. You
thought of going to the trading post for water. Your
grandfather went once a week, and sometimes twice, in
the wagon; and if he didn't need the water right away,
he waited for you to bring the sheep in, and you went
with him. He didn't like to leave the sheep alone, but it
was only for a little while, and he knew how much you
wanted to go. The water was low in the barrel; you had
looked inside the night before and there was only
enough for the morning. You thought about the road,
the hillsides and the way through the flats, and you
hoped the snow wouldn't melt too soon into mud. It
would be all right; it wasn't like the long hard rains. It
would be all right if you didn't stay out too long with
the sheep. You hurried and looked hard for the grass.
And afterward, when you brought the sheep back, your
grandfather had filled the barrel with snow and there
was plenty of water again. But he took you to the
trading post anyway, because you were little and had
looked forward to it. There were people inside, a lot of
them, because there was a big snow on the ground and
they needed things and they wanted to stand around
and smoke and talk about the weather. You were little
and there was a lot to see, and all of it was new and
beautiful: bright new buckets and tubs, saddles and
ropes, hats and shirts and boots, a big glass case all
filled with candy. Frazer was the trader's name. He
gave you a piece of hard red candy and laughed because you couldn't make up your mind to take it at
first, and you wanted it so much you didn't know what
to do. And he gave your grandfather some tobacco and
brown paper. And when he had smoked, your grandfather talked to the trader for a long time and you didn't*

know what they were saying and you just looked around at all the new and beautiful things. And after a while the trader put some things out on the counter, sacks of flour and sugar, a slab of salt pork, some canned goods, and a little bag full of the hard red candy. And your grandfather took off one of his rings and gave it to the trader. It was a small green stone, set carelessly in thin silver. It was new and it wasn't worth very much, not all the trader gave for it anyway. And the trader opened one of the cans, a big can of whole tomatoes, and your grandfather sprinkled sugar on the tomatoes and the two of you ate them right there and drank bottles of sweet red soda pop. And it was getting late and you rode home in the sunset and the whole land was cold and white. And that night your grandfather hammered the strips of silver and told you stories in the firelight. And you were little and right there in the center of everything, the sacred mountains, the snow-covered mountains and the hills, the gullies and the flats, the sundown and the night, everything— where you were little, where you were and had to be.

It was kind of hard for him, you know, getting used to everything. We had to get down there pretty early and put in a day's work. And then at night we would go down to Henry's place and fool around. We would get drunk and have a good time. There were always some girls down there, and on paydays we acted pretty big.

But he was unlucky. Everything went along all right for about two months, I guess. And it would have gone all right after that, too, if they had just let him alone. Maybe . . . you never know about a guy like that; but they wouldn't let him alone. The parole officer, and welfare, and the Relocation people kept coming around, you know, and they were always after him about something. They wanted to know how he was doing, had he been staying out of trouble, and all. I guess that got on his nerves after a while, especially the business about drinking and running around. They were always *warning* him, you know? Telling him how he had to stay out of trouble, or else he was going to wind up in prison again. I guess he had to think about that all the time, because they wouldn't let him forget it. Sometimes they talked to me about him, too, and I said he was getting along all right. But he wasn't. And I could see why, but I didn't know how to tell them about it. They wouldn't have understood anyway. You have to get *used* to everything, you know; it's like starting out someplace where you've never been before, and you don't know where you're going or why or when you have to get there, and everybody's looking at you, waiting for you, wondering why you don't hurry up. And they can't help you because you don't know how to talk to them. They have a lot of *words,* and you know they mean something, but you don't know what, and your own words are no good because they're not the same; they're different, and they're the only words you've got. Everything is different, and you don't know how to get used to it. You see the way it is, how everything is going on without you, and you start to worry about it. You wonder how you can get yourself into the swing of it, you know? And you don't know how, but you've got to do it because there's nothing else. And you *want* to do it, because you can see how good it is. It's better than anything you've ever had; it's money and clothes and having plans and going someplace fast. You can see what it's like, but you don't know how to get into it; there's too much of it and it's all around you and you can't get hold of it because it's going on too fast. You have to get used to it first, and it's hard. You've got to be left alone. You've got to put a lot of things out of your mind, or you're going to get all mixed up. You've got to take it easy and get drunk once in a while and just forget about who you are. It's hard, and you want to give up. You think about getting out and going home. You want to think that you belong someplace, I guess. You go up there on the hill and you hear the singing and the talk and you think about going home. But the next day you know it's no use; you know that if you went home there would be nothing there, just the empty land and a lot of old people, going noplace and dying off. And you've got to forget about that, too. Well, they were always coming around and warning him. They wouldn't let him alone, and pretty soon I could see that he was getting all mixed up.

There was some trouble down at the plant. We were shorthanded for a while, and we had to put in a lot of overtime. Daniels—he's the foreman—was getting pretty nervous, I guess, because a lot of orders were coming in, and we were running pretty far behind. He's a hard man to work for anyway—he's all business, you know, and he won't stand for any fooling around on the job—but he was *really* worried about that time, and he was watching us pretty close and getting on us pretty bad.

One night after we had worked a twelve-hour day, we went over to Tosamah's place and got up a poker game. There were five or six of us, I guess, and we were all drinking a lot and having fun. We had to get up early the next day, and after a while I started to worry about the time. It was getting late, and I was dead tired. He was tired, too, and the liquor was getting to him. He didn't know Tosamah very well, and Tosamah was feeling pretty good, going on about everything, you know, and talking big. Well, I could tell that he didn't like it much; it was getting on his nerves. I kept telling him that we ought to go on back home and get some sleep, but he wouldn't listen to me. He just kept on sitting there, listening to Tosamah go on about everything and getting more and more drunk. I guess Tosamah knew what he was thinking, too, because pretty soon he started in on him; not directly, you know, but he started talking about *longhairs* and the reservation and all. I kept wishing he would shut up, and I guess the others did, too—all except Cruz; he was just grinning like a fool—because right away they got quiet and just started looking down at their hands, you know, like they were trying to decide what to do. I knew that something bad was going to happen.

You know, some people smile when they get mad, and the madder they get the more they smile. He was like that. He just sat there and smiled, and that was a bad sign, but I guess nobody knew it but me. I knew there was going to be some trouble, and I was getting scared. And, sure enough, pretty soon he just flew off the handle. It was like everything just exploded inside of him, and he jumped up from the table and started for Tosamah. But he was crazy drunk, and he couldn't stay on his feet. He stumbled backward and fell against the sink. He was looking for Tosamah, and it was a bad, scary look, but he couldn't get his eyes to hold still, you know, and he couldn't move. He just leaned there, trying to get hold of himself, and shaking all over like he was having a kind of coughing fit or something. It all happened real quick, and Cruz started to laugh, and then the others did, too; and that seemed to take all the fight out of him. It was like he had to give up when they laughed; it was like all of a sudden he didn't care about anything anymore. You know, at the time I was glad it ended up like that, because if there had been a fight they would have blamed it on him. But I got to thinking afterward that he was hurt by what had happened; he was hurt inside somehow, and pretty bad.

He didn't go to work the next day, or the next. I couldn't get him to go, and he wouldn't even talk to me. He was ashamed, I guess, or maybe he thought I was mad at him. Right away Daniels wanted to know where he was, and I said he was sick. He didn't say anything, Daniels, but just swore a couple of times and left me alone. I'm pretty sure he didn't believe me. The orders kept coming in and we weren't catching up at all.

He was passed out when I got home. He stayed drunk for two days. He didn't go anywhere; he just stayed up here in the room, I guess, and drank himself sick. I guess I knew then that he was going to lose that job, and I felt pretty bad, because he needed it. It was a good job, and he could handle it all right. But, sure enough, when he went back Daniels was looking out for him. He came over to the line and just stood there, looking over his shoulder, you know, inspecting everything he did. Now you know it's hard to work like that, with somebody important watching you all the time, and I could see that he was starting to sweat. He made a couple of mistakes, and Daniels got on him right away. They weren't anything to get excited about, just some loose or crooked staples, but Daniels acted like it was a big thing, and he was talking loud and calling attention to it. Well, that was more than he could take, I guess; Daniels had been riding him all morning, and pretty soon he just got enough of it. Finally he just dropped everything and looked at Daniels hard, like maybe he was going to hit him or something, and walked out. I guess that took Daniels by surprise, because he just stood there for a minute with his mouth open. And then he was really burned up, you know, and he went running all around like he didn't know what to do and yelling about "these damned no-good greasers" and all. But I think he felt kind of foolish, too. We were shorthanded, and it takes time to find and train a good man like that. Well, he had no right to stand over him that way and call attention to his mistakes. We were doing all right; we were getting the job done.

He went downhill pretty fast after that. Sometimes he was here when I came in from work, and sometimes he wasn't. He was drunk about half the time, and I couldn't keep up with him. I tried to get him to slow down, you know, but he just got mad whenever I said anything about it, and it made him worse. Right away his money ran out, and he started hitting me up for a loan every night, almost. Pretty soon I wouldn't give him any more, but you know what he did? He started asking Milly for money. He would tell her he needed some new clothes, or bus fare to look for a job or something, and she would give him two or three dollars, sometimes five, every time. And he would just blow it in on liquor right away. I told her what he was doing, but she said she knew it; she just felt sorry for him. The Relocation people got him a job with the schools, taking care of the grounds and all, but he showed up drunk a couple of times and they fired him after the first week and a half. Milly got him a job, too; it was a night job at some bakery, and she said the pay was pretty good. But he didn't even bother to show up for it. You know, if he could just have held on the first time, to that first job down there on my line, he might have been all right. We liked each other, and we worked pretty well together. I could kind of keep an eye on him down there, you know, look out for him, and that was good. I guess he needed somebody to look out for him. Nobody but Milly and me gave a damn what happened to him.

We had some good times—a few, even after that. Sometimes Milly would come around in the morning on Sundays, and she would bring a basket with maybe some sandwiches and Kool-Aid and apples and cookies inside. And we would get on the bus, the three of us, and go all the way out to Santa Monica. We would find us some place out there on the beach where there weren't too many people, you know, and we would just sit around down there in the sun and talk and kid each other and look at the swimmers and the birds and the ocean. Milly had a little white swimsuit, and she always brought it along, and sometimes she would go out in the water and we would watch her. I felt kind of funny when she was dressed like that, and, you know, he would make jokes and say things about her sometimes, and I laughed all right, but I didn't like it much, because I thought a lot of her and she was good to us. I never said anything when he talked like that. It would have been worse if I had, because he would have made fun of me, you know, and said I had some plans with her and all. It wasn't like that. She liked him better than me, I think, and I was always afraid that he might hurt her somehow. She was easy-going and friendly to everybody. She *trusted* everybody, I guess; some people are just like that. And she had had a hard time all her life. It would have been pretty easy to hurt her.

Sometimes when we went out like that, the three of us, she would tell us about her family and all, how it was when she was little. She was raised on a farm someplace, and I guess her people had it pretty hard. She talked about her dad a lot. He had worked himself to death on that farm, she said, trying to get things to grow. The ground was no good, and nothing much ever came out of it. He had to work a long time just to get enough money so she could go to school. She said she always meant to pay him back, but he died before she could do it.

She fell in love with some guy and they were married for a while. She only talked about that once, and all she said was that everything was all right for a little while, better than it had ever been. Then right away she started talking about something else. It was like she was going to cry, you know; you could tell that something bad had happened. But she talked about good things, too. She was always remembering something funny, and she laughed a lot. I never knew anybody who was always ready to laugh like that. And she was always getting us to laugh, too. You could see how easy it would be to hurt her.

No, wait a minute. There was someone who laughed, who was ready to laugh, whose eyes were laughing. Yes, one summer there was a girl at Cornfields, yes.

And pretty soon she would get us talking, too. We felt kind of free and easy with her, you know, and we told her things we wouldn't tell to just anybody. We didn't mean to, exactly; it just happened that way, because she was always laughing and kind of open, you know, and you could see that she wasn't making fun of you. We used to tell her about the reservation, and it was all right, you know, because we made a kind of joke out of it; we talked about the funny things that had happened to us. One day it was like that, and we were just sitting around down there in the sand and looking out at the water. It had been kind of cold and foggy all that week, but that day was clear and warm, and we were feeling good and kind of lazy out there. Milly had been in the water, and she came over and sat down between us. Her hair was wet and she was laughing and there were beads of water all over her face and arms and legs. She looked real pretty that way, you know, all clean and cool and fresh-looking. Her skin was white and clean, and she put her feet down under the sand and wiggled her toes. He had been trying for a couple of days to straighten himself out, talking about getting a job and all. Milly believed him, and I guess I did, too. Anyway, we were having a good time, the three of us, laughing and kidding around and talking about all kinds of things.

Somehow we got to talking about horses. He was telling us about a horse he used to have. It was a good one, small and fast, you know, but it hadn't been broken all the way. It acted kind of wild sometimes, and it had a mean streak in it, like a mule. That horse liked the water, he said. It always wanted to go, to take out for the river. It would get away sometimes, and he would have to go looking for it. And he always found it in the same place, just standing there in the river, looking around like everything was just the way it ought to be. Well, one day he was riding that horse back from the fields, and he came across some old man. That old man was important, somehow; he was a governor or a medicine man or something. He was real *dignified*, you know, and he never smiled. Well, he wanted a ride. He said O.K., and he took that old man up on the horse behind him. They started out all right, but they had to cross the river. And when they got right in the middle of the river, that crazy horse just decided to lie down and that old man fell off in the river. He was old, and I guess he thought that was the damnedest horse he had ever seen. He got up, you know, and he was looking kind of bad, like a wet hen. He didn't say a word; he just shook his head and walked off. And his shoes were all full of water, and you could hear him squeak along for quite a while.

When Milly heard that, the way he told it, she got so tickled she didn't know what to do. She couldn't stop laughing, and pretty soon we had to laugh, too. And then she got the hiccups, and that just made it worse. We almost laughed ourselves sick. We were just sitting there shaking and the tears were coming out of our eyes and we were acting like a bunch of damn fools, I guess, and we didn't care. She was pretty when she laughed.

There was a girl at Cornfields one summer.

Milly believed him, you know, because she wanted to believe everybody; she was like that, and she made us believe it, too, that everything was going to be all right, and we were happy and making some plans about how it was going to be.

Pony, they called her, and she laughed, and her skin was light and she had long little hands and she wore a dark blue velveteen blouse and a corn-blossom necklace with an old najahe like the moon and one perfect powder-blue stone. . . .

I guess he believed it. But it wasn't going to be like that. It wasn't going to turn out right, because it was too late; everything had gone too far with him, you know, and he was already sick inside. Maybe he was sick a long time, always, and nobody knew it, and it was just coming out for the first time and you could see it. It might have been like that.

There was a girl at Cornfields one summer, and she laughed, and you never saw her again. You had been away at school, and it was the first time you were homesick and it was good to be out there again. It looked just the same, like the land was going on forever and nothing had changed. You got off the bus at Chambers and walked all the way to the trading post at Wide Ruins, and you weren't used to walking way out like that and it took a long time and it was hot and you were tired. You went in there to get a cold drink, and old man Frazer acted like he was glad to see you. And

*you were feeling pretty big, because you had been away
and you figured you had seen what there was to see. It
was hot, and it was getting on toward late afternoon,
and you didn't feel much like walking the rest of the
way home. You were kind of hoping that your grandfather might be coming for water, but Frazer said that he
had been there the day before. You were glad just to be
inside where it was cool, and Frazer acted like he was
glad to see you, and the two of you stood around
talking about everything. He said there was going to be
a squaw dance near cornfields the next night. And you
hadn't been to a squaw dance in a long time. It sounded good to you, and right away you wanted to go. You
were feeling pretty big, and you started trading with
Frazer just like an old-timer, kind of slow and easy,
like you didn't care much about it. And after a while
you asked him if he had any good horses for sale. He
had a good black, he said, but it was worth a lot of
money and he didn't figure to sell it right away. You
just nodded and let it go for a while, but then you told
him you had an uncle over there west of Cornfields
who had a fine old ketoh that he was going to give you.
He had had it for a long time, you said, and it was
good work; there was a great spider web in the center
and a circle of little matching ones all around, and the
silver was heavy and thick. But it was old, you said, the
kind you didn't see around much anymore. And you
acted like that was too bad, it being so old and out of
style, and right away you could see that he was thinking about it hard. He asked you when you were going
to get it, and you acted like you hadn't thought much
about it and said maybe if you went to that squaw
dance you would talk to your uncle about it. And then
he asked you what you were going to do with it when
you got it. Well, you said, you didn't know for sure.
you didn't see things like that anymore. You guessed
you would hold on to it for a while and see what
happened. And that's when he said, "Come on, let me
show you that horse; it's a good one." It was, too. It*

was a pretty little black, all sleek and round and long-legged. It looked like it could run. It looked kind of slow, you said, and lazy, like maybe it wasn't getting enough exercise. Maybe you would buy that horse, you said, but first you would have to try it out for a couple of days. If he wanted, you said, you would ride that horse out to Cornfields and try to get the ketoh. *He said no at first, but you went on about your uncle, how the trader at Ganado had seen that* ketoh *and wanted to buy it, and finally he got a bridle and led the horse out and put the reins in your hand.*

The black horse felt good under you, and you let it lope all the way out to your grandfather's place. The sun was going down and the land was red and a little wind was getting up and it was cool and you were home again.

It's going to rain all night, I guess. It's cold and rainy up there on the hill, and nobody's there. It's dark and quiet and muddy up there. It will be muddy for a long time. He wanted me to tell him how it was going to be, you know. It's funny how it can be so clear like that one night and rain the next, and go on raining like it wasn't ever going to stop. Maybe he's out of it, you know? He's way out there someplace by now, and maybe it isn't raining and he's awake and he can see the stars and the moonlight on the land. The train will slow down and begin to climb the mountains around Williams and Flagstaff and the moonlight will be all over the trees and you can see the black trees against the sky. Maybe he's awake and all right.

And then the train will head south and east and down on the land, and the sun will come up out there and you can see a long way out across the land. You can see the sun coming up on the Painted Desert and the dark gullies and the red and purple earth in the early morning, all beautiful and still, and the land reaching out toward Wide Ruins and Klagetoh and Cornfields.

You felt good out there, like everything was all right and still and cool inside you, and that black horse loping along like the wind. Your grandfather was another year older and he cried; he cried because your mother and father were dead and he had raised you and you had gone away and you were coming home. You were coming home like a man, on a black and beautiful horse. He sang about it. It was all right, everything, and there was nothing to say.

You were tired then, and you went to sleep thinking of the morning. And at first light you went out and knew where you were. And it was the same, the way you remembered it, the way you knew it had to be; and nothing had changed. The first light, you thought, that little while before sunup; it would always be the same out there. That was the way it was, that's all. It was that way on the day you were born, and it would be that way on the day you died. It was cold, and you could feel the cold on your face and hands. The clouds were the same, smoky and small and far away, and the land was dark and still and it went all around to the sky. Nothing could fill it but the sun that was coming up, and then it would be bright, brighter than water, and the brightness would be made of a hundred colors and the land would almost hurt your eyes. But at first light it was soft and gray and very still. There was no sound, nothing. The sky was waiting all around, and the east was white, like a shell. At first light the land was alone and very still. And you were there where you wanted to be, and alone. You didn't want to see anyone, or hear anyone speak. There was nothing to say..

The sun came up behind you and you rode the black horse out on the way to Cornfields. It was a good horse, all right, better than most. It was deep and wide in the chest, and long-winded. It could go on loping and loping like that all the way if you wanted to hurry. But it was early enough, and you didn't have far to go, half a day's ride and a little more. You could see the earth going away under you, and you could feel and

*hear the hoofs. It was early enough, and the heat was
holding off; and the black horse carried you just hard
enough into the slow morning air. It was good going
out like that, and it made you want to pray.*

I am the Turquoise Woman's son.
On top of Belted Mountain,
Beautiful horse—slim like a weasel.
My horse has a hoof like striped agate;
His fetlock is like a fine eagle plume;
His legs are like quick lightning.
My horse's body is like an eagle-plumed arrow;
My horse has a tail like a trailing black cloud.
I put flexible goods on my horse's back;
The Little Holy Wind blows through his hair.
His mane is made of short rainbows.
My horse's ears are made of round corn.
My horse's eyes are made of big stars.
My horse's head is made of mixed waters—
From the holy waters—he never knows thirst.
My horse's teeth are made of white shell.
The long rainbow is in his mouth for a bridle,
      and with it I guide him.
When my horse neighs, different-colored horses
      follow.
When my horse neighs, different-colored sheep
      follow.
  I am wealthy, because of him.
  Before me peaceful,
  Behind me peaceful,
  Under me peaceful,
  Over me peaceful,
  All around me peaceful—
  Peaceful voice when he neighs.
I am Everlasting and Peaceful.
I stand for my horse.

*You went up by Klagetoh, to the trading post there,
and spent the early afternoon inside, talking and laughing, boasting of the black horse, until the sun was low*

and it was cool again. You rode on to Sam Charley's place, and he went the rest of the way with you. And the two of you laughed and made jokes about the girls at school—the Nambé girls and Apaches—and Sam Charley's horse was old and used to work. It was a poor thing beside the black, and the black horse danced around and threw its head and wanted to run. There was no ketoh, but the black horse was yours for a while and you were riding it out to Cornfields and that was all that mattered.

And there, afterward, a little way west of Cornfields, the sun was going down and the sunset was deep and purple on the sky and the night fell with cold. And there were wagons and fires, and you could hear the talk and smell the smoke and the coffee and the fried bread. And there was a spotted moon coming up in the east, like a concho hammered out thin and deep in the center. And the drums. You heard the drums, and you wished you were still on the way and alone, miles away, where you could hear the drums and see only the moonlight on the land and then at last the fires a long way off. You can hear the drums a long way on the land at night and you don't know where they are until you see the fires, because the drums are all around on the land, going on and on for miles, and then you come over a hill and suddenly there they are, the fires and the drums, and still they sound far away.

They began the dance and you stood away and watched. There was a girl on the other side, and she was laughing and beautiful, and it was good to look at her. The firelight moved on her skin and she was laughing. The firelight shone on the blue velveteen of her blouse and on the pale new moon najahe of the corn blossom. And after a while you watched her all the time when she wasn't looking, because you saw slowly how beautiful she was. She was slender and small; she moved a little to the drums, standing in place, and her long skirt swayed at her feet and there were dimes on her moccasins.

"*Hey, hosteen.*" Sam Charley's hand was on your shoulder. "*She has her eye on you. She's thinking it over.*"

"*That is a fine necklace,*" you said. "*Who is she?*"

"*Ei yei! It's a fine necklace! Maybe you want to give her something for it, huh? They call her Pony. She lives over yonder by Naslini, I think.*"

And after a while there were many couples dancing around the fires. They passed slowly in front of you, under their blankets, holding hands, stepping out lightly to the drums, the shapes of their bodies close together and dark against the fires. And you lost sight of her. You looked all around, but she was gone. Sam Charley said something, but you couldn't hear what it was; you could hear only the drums, going on like the beat of your heart. And then she was holding on to your arm, laughing, and she said, "*Come on, or give me something that is worth a lot of money.*" Her laughter was a certain thing; it made you careless and sure of yourself, and you wanted always to hear it. She gave you her blanket and led you out in the open by the fires. And you let the blanket fall over your back and you held it open to her and she stepped inside of it. She was small and close beside you, laughing, and you held her for a long time in the dance. You went slowly together, slowly in time around the fires, and she was laughing beside you and the moon was high and the drums were going on far out into the night and the black horse was tethered close by in the camps and the moon and the fires shone upon the dark blue velvet of its rump and flanks and your hand lay upon dark blue velvet and looking down you saw the little footsteps of the girl licking out upon the firelit sand, the small white angles of the soles and the deep red sheaths and the shining silver dimes. And you never saw her again.

We were coming home one night from Henry's place. We had been standing around outside with a lot of other guys, and we were talking pretty loud and having a big time, you know, but after a while it broke

up, and it was late and we decided to come on home.
We were just walking along kind of slow and talking
pretty loud, I guess, and the street was dark and empty.
There's an alley down there. It's a dead end and empty,
except for a pile of used lumber and some garbage
cans. It's always dark in there at night because the
nearest streetlight is down at the end of the block.
There are a lot of pigeons in there in the daytime,
because people are always throwing things away in
there; there's always a lot of cans and broken glass and
stuff lying around, and it smells pretty bad. Well, we
were going by that alley, and Martinez stepped out in
front of us. He just stood there at first, tapping that
stick in his hand and looking at us. He made us jump,
coming out of that dark alley like that, and right away
we shut up, you know, and I was scared. Then he told
us to go into the alley, and he followed us. I was sober
right away; it was dark in there and he was close and I
could barely see him. I didn't know what he was going
to do, and I was scared and shaking.

"Hello, Benally," he said, real soft and easy like. I
couldn't see his face, but I knew he was smiling the
way he does when he knows you're scared. We were
just going home, I said, and I asked him what he
wanted. He just stood there, smiling and watching us
sweat, I guess, and all the time tapping that stick in his
hand. "Let's see your hands, Benally." He was close to
us, and we had our backs to the wall. I raised my
hands up and held them out. I was almost touching
him. He had a flashlight, you know, and he turned it
on. "Your hands, Benally, they're shaking," he said,
like he wondered why and was worried about it. He
made me keep my hands there for a long time in the
bright light, and they were shaking bad and I couldn't
hold them still. Then he asked me how much money I
had. He knew I had been paid, I guess, and I gave him
all I had left. He looked at the money for a long time,
like maybe it wasn't enough, and I was scared and
shaking. Pretty soon, "Hello," he said. "Who's your
friend, Benally?" And he stepped in front of him and

held the light up to his face. I told him his name and
said he was out of work; he was looking for a job and
didn't have any money. Martinez told him to hold out
his hands, and he did, slowly, like maybe he wasn't
going to at first, with the palms up. I could see his
hands in the light and they were open and almost
steady. "Turn them over," Martinez said, and he was
looking at them and they were almost steady. Then
suddenly the light jumped and he brought the stick
down hard and fast. I couldn't see it, but I heard it
crack on the bones of the hands, and it made me sick.
He didn't cry out or make a sound, but I could see him
there against the wall, doubled up with pain and holding his hands. And the light went out and Martinez
went by me in the dark, and I could hear him breathe,
short and quick, like he was laughing, you know. We
got out of there and went on home. His hands weren't
broken, but they were swollen up pretty bad and the
next day he could barely move his fingers and there
were big ugly marks above his knuckles, all yellow
and purple. We told Milly that we had been working on
that radiator, you know, and it fell over on his hands.

He couldn't forget about it. It was like that time at
Tosamah's place, you know? He didn't say anything—
and even when it happened he didn't say anything; he
just doubled over down there against the wall and held
his hands—but he couldn't forget about it. He would
sit around, looking down all the time at his hands.
Sometimes I would say something, and it was like he
didn't hear me, like he had something bad on his mind
and he had to do something but he didn't know what it
was. Then he would look up after a while and ask me
what I had said. It was getting harder and harder to
talk to him. Milly would say something funny, you
know, and she and I would laugh and look at him, and
he would smile, but you could tell that he was thinking
about something else and hadn't heard. And even when
he got drunk it was different somehow. He used to get
drunk and happy, and we would laugh and kid around
a lot, but after that night it was different.

One day I came by for him and we went out to Westwood. Sometimes, when I'm pretty well caught up on the line, Daniels lets me take the truck out on a delivery. It's a nice break, you know, because you get a chance to see everything and get some fresh air. When there wasn't a big hurry and I had to go way out someplace like that, I would take him along. Daniels never found out, or I guess I would have been fired. Well, it was a nice day, and he was just sitting around up here, like he didn't know what to do, so I told him to come on and he seemed pretty glad to go. We went out on Wilshire, and it was a nice day and it was getting on toward noon. I didn't have to be back until one, and it was only going to take a few minutes to unload. I figured when I was through we would have time to get a hamburger and drive down by the beach. I always liked Westwood, and it was a nice day and there were a lot of people walking around on the streets. I backed the truck into the alley and pulled up to the dock. The cab was out a little way on the sidewalk, and the people had to go around. He waited in the cab while I unloaded. It wasn't a big order, and I was through pretty quick. I got back in the truck and started to pull out, but he told me to wait. "Let's go," I said. We just had time to beat the noon-hour traffic on Wilshire and get on down to the beach. But he made me wait, and we were just sitting there, you know, and I didn't know what was going on and I was getting kind of mad. Pretty soon a woman came out of one of the shops, and he nodded and wanted me to look at her. She was all dressed up and just walking along kind of slow and looking in the windows. She passed right in front of us, you know, and he leaned back a little like he didn't want her to see him. I didn't know what was going on. She was good-looking, all right, but she wasn't young or big anywhere and I couldn't see anything to get excited about. She was rich-looking and kind of slim; you could tell that she had been out in the sun and her skin was kind of golden, you know, and she had on a plain white dress and little white shoes

and gloves. She was good-looking, all right. She had on
sunglasses, and her mouth was small and pretty with
some kind of pale color on her lips, and her hair wasn't
long but it was neat and shiny and clean-looking; there
was one streak of silver in it, clean and wide, and all
around it the dark, shining hair, almost copper-colored
in the sun. We watched her out of sight.

He said he knew her. He used to work for her, I
guess, and she liked him. She was going to help him, he
said. She liked him a lot, and, you know, they fooled
around and everything, and she was going to help him
get a job and go away from the reservation, but then he
got himself in trouble. He kept saying that: that she
liked him and was going to help him some way, but he
got himself in trouble. I didn't believe him at first, and
I was kind of mad because he was going on like that,
bragging and joking about some white woman. But I
found out later that he was telling the truth. When he
got hurt, you know, he talked about her and said her
name, and he was hurt bad and out of his mind, and
you could tell that he wasn't making it up. It's funny,
but even at first, when I thought he was kidding
around, he acted somehow like he knew all about her
and she was special and good and she liked him a lot. I
saw her again at the hospital. She was good-looking, all
right, like those women you see in the magazines.

He didn't look for a job anymore.

I wish we had remembered to close that window.
Rain. I wish it would stop raining. This place is always
cold and kind of empty when it rains. We were going to
tear out some pictures of horses and cars and boats and
put them up on the walls. Milly brought some curtains
over one time, but we never did get around to putting
them up. Maybe I'll put them up tomorrow. She'd get a
kick out of that. We used to kid him about that little
suitcase. It was over there in the corner, and there was
one little spider that always wanted to make a web
across it. Milly would come in and brush it away, but
that little spider got right to work and made another
web in the same place. It never gave up, and finally we

told her to leave it alone. That spider was our roommate, we said, and she didn't have any right to come around all the time, trying to evict it. Then she was always talking about how nobody, even a spider, ought to live in a suitcase and she was going to bring some tin shears and make a doll house out of it; that spider ought to have a little rocking chair, she said. It gets cold in here when it rains. It's a good place; you could fix it up real nice. There are a lot of good places around here. I could find some place with a private bathroom if I wanted to, easy. A man with a good job can do just about anything he wants.

Old Carlozini ought to be getting home pretty soon. She's old, and she ought not to be out in the rain like that. One of these days she's going to just fall down and die in the street, or they're going to find her all alone in that little room of hers. She has a few little things, you know, some dishes and spoons, and every morning about five-thirty you can hear her moving around down there. She always wears that old black hat when she goes out. It looks funny on her because it's big and the brim droops down all around her head and there's an old beat-up flower that hangs down over one eye and bounces around when she walks. She never says hello or anything, but she's always watching you, like maybe she thinks you're going to sneak up on her or steal something from her. She can hear you on the stairs, you know, and she always opens her door a little, just a crack, and watches you go by. That's about all she has to do, I guess.

One time we were going out, and old Carlozini was sitting down there on the stairs, all bent over and still, like she was going to sleep. The door of her room was wide open, and she was just sitting out there on the stairs, and it was the first time we had ever seen the inside of her room. It was real dark and dirty-looking, and even out there on the stairs we could smell it. I guess it was the first time that door had ever been left open like that. She never takes a bath, and you know how old people smell and how they like to shut them-

selves up in the dark. It was pretty bad, that smell.
Well, we started to go around her and she said something. We turned and she was looking up at us and her
eyes were all wet. "Vincenzo is not well," she said. "It
is very bad this time." She had a little cardboard box in
her hands and she held it out to us. We didn't know
what she was talking about, but we looked inside that
box and there was a little dead animal of some kind, a
guinea pig, I guess; it had black and white fur and it
was kind of curled up on its side and there was a dirty
white cloth under it. "Oh, it is very bad this time," she
said, and she was shaking her head. We didn't know
what to say, and she was crying and looking at us like
maybe we could make it all right if we wanted to. It
was like she was being real friendly and nice to us, you
know, so we would make it all right. "His name is
Vincenzo," she said. "He's very smart, you know; he
can stand up straight, just like you gentlemen, and clap
his little hands." And her eyes lit up and she had to
smile, thinking about it. She went on like that, like that
little thing was still alive and maybe it was going to
stand up and clap its hands like a baby. It made me
real sad to see her, so old and lonely and carrying on
like that, and she kept saying "you gentlemen" and
everything. We didn't know what to do, and we just
listened to her and looked down at that little furry
animal. And then after a while he said he thought it
was dead. At first I thought he shouldn't have said that;
it seemed kind of mean somehow, you know? But I
guess she had to be told. I think maybe she knew it was
dead all the time, and she was just waiting for someone
to say it, because she didn't know how to say it herself.
All at once she jerked that little box away and looked
at him real hard for a minute, like she was hurt and
couldn't understand how it was, why on earth he
should say a thing like that. But then she just nodded
and slumped over a little bit. She didn't say any more,
and she wasn't crying; it was like she was real tired,
you know, and didn't have any strength left. I asked
her if she wanted us to take Vincenzo out to the alley,

but she just sat there and didn't say anything. She was just sitting there on the stairs, holding that little dead animal real close to her, and she looked awful small and alone and the night was coming on and it was getting dark down there. It's funny, you know; that little animal was her friend, I guess, and she kept it down there in her room, always, maybe, and we didn't even know about it. And afterward it was just the same. She never said anything to us again.

There's always a lot of rain this time of the year. It isn't bad; it lets up after a while, and then everything is bright and clean. It's a good place to live. There's always a lot going on, a lot of things to do and see once you find your way around. Once you find your way around and get used to everything, you wonder how you ever got along out there where you came from. There's nothing there, you know, just the land, and the land is empty and dead. Everything is here, everything you could ever want. You never have to be alone. You go downtown and there are a lot of people all around, and they're having a good time. You see how it is with them, how they get along and have money and nice things, radios and cars and clothes and big houses. And you want those things; you'd be crazy not to want them. And you can have them, too; they're so *easy* to have. You go down to those stores, and they're full of bright new things and you can buy just about anything you want. The people are real friendly most of the time, and they're always ready to help you out. They don't even know you, but they're friendly anyway; they go out of their way to be nice. They shake your hand and pay attention to you; and sometimes you don't know how to act, you know, but they try to make it easy for you. It's like they *want* you to get along, like they're looking out for you. The Relocation people are all right, too. It's not like Tosamah says. They know how it is when you first come, how scared you are and all, and they look out for you. They pay your way; they get you a job and a place to stay; I guess they even take

care of you if you get sick. You don't have to worry
about a thing.

"No, sirree, Benally, you don't have to worry about a
thing." That's what Tosamah says. He's always going
on about Relocation and Welfare and Termination and
all, and that little fat Cruz is always right behind him,
smiling and nodding like he knew what it was all
about. I used to listen to Tosamah. He's a clown, and
you have to laugh at some of the things he says. But
you have to know how to take it, too. He likes to get
under your skin; he'll make a fool out of you if you let
him.

Let's see . . . let's see; Manygoats gave me three
dollars, and I bought a bottle of wine. I wonder who
that great big girl was. I have two dollars and eleven
cents. I wish I had some more of that wine. I wish I
had another bottle of wine . . . and a dollar bill . . . and
two dimes . . . and two pennies.

*Ei yeil with a name like that, and she had dimes . . .
dimes on her shoes.*

She's from Oklahoma, I think.

*Henry, you keep that dollar bill and those two pen-
nies. Give me twelve shiny dimes. For old time's sake,
Henry, give me twelve shiny dimes. Time's dimes, shine
wine.*

Maybe the rain will let up for a while.

He didn't look for a job anymore. It's funny, you
know? Everything happened real fast. We had a fight. I
couldn't talk to him. He was always drunk. We used to
get drunk together, and it was all right because it made
us loose and happy and we could kid around and forget
about things. But after a while, after that night when
Martinez . . . or maybe it was before that; I don't know.
Maybe it was Tosamah, too, and that white woman,
everything. But it wasn't fun anymore. The liquor
didn't seem to make any difference; he was just the
same, sitting around and looking down like he hated
everything, like he hated himself and hated being drunk

and hated Milly and me, and I couldn't talk to him. Every time I tried to say anything, he just got mad. It had to stop, you know? I could see that something real bad was going to happen if it didn't stop, but I couldn't do anything. He wouldn't let anybody help him, and I guess I got mad, too, and one day we had a fight. He was crazy drunk and ugly. He had thrown up all over himself, and he couldn't do anything about it, I guess, and he was just sitting there and saying the worst thing he could think of, over and over. I didn't like to hear that kind of talk, you know; it made me kind of scared, and I told him to cut it out. I guess I was more scared than mad; anyway, I had had about all I could take. I was tired of worrying about him all the time, and he was getting worse and something bad was going to happen and I didn't want any part of it. He just went on and it was worse and he was mad and snarling those things at me, and I was sick of it and I told him to get out. Pretty soon he got up and staggered around and he was all red and sweaty and shaking, and he was looking wild, you know, and I didn't care because I was mad. O.K., he said, that was it, and I could go to hell and he was leaving. He was going out to look for *culebra,* he said; he was going to get even with *culebra,* and I told him to go ahead, I didn't give a damn. He went out and slammed the door, and I was glad, and I could hear him on the stairs, like he was crazy and was going to fall and hurt himself, and I didn't care.

I cooled off, and right away I was sorry and I started to worry about him. But I figured it didn't do any good. It had to stop, you know; something had to happen. He didn't come back, and I was worried. I waited up for a long time, and it was getting late. I had a hard time going to sleep. I kept listening for him, but he didn't come back. I kept telling myself that maybe it was a good thing, him going out by himself like that. He was drunk and sick, you know, and he couldn't get very far. I figured maybe he had been picked up and thrown in jail; maybe they could see that he was sick and they would get a doctor to take care of him. He didn't come back that night, and the next day I had to go to work and I was glad to be busy. I worked hard on the line, and it was like everything was all right. He would be there when I got home, and we would straighten everything out.

He didn't come back for three days. I went right home from work every day and he wasn't there. I kept going down to Henry's place and all around, back and forth, and nobody had seen him. He wasn't in jail. I didn't know what to do. Then, three nights later, I woke up and heard something down there on the stairs. I went out and turned on the light in the hall, and I could see him down there in the dark at the foot of the stairs, like he was dead. Old Carlozini's door was open just a crack, and she was looking out at him. The light from her room made a line across him, and he was all twisted up and still. It was him, all right, and he was almost dead. I thought he was dead, and I didn't know what to do. I ran down there and I couldn't think and I forgot about that light not working and I tried to turn it on. I yelled at that old woman to open her door, but she just stood there, and I had to push her out of the way; I pushed hard, and maybe she fell—I don't know but I got that door open. He was lying there on his stomach and I turned him over and I wanted to get sick and cry. He was all broken and torn and covered with blood. Most of the blood was dry; it had dried up on his clothes and in his hair. He had lost an awful lot of blood, and his skin was pale yellow in the light. His eyes were swollen shut and his nose was broken and his mouth was raw and bleeding. And his hands were broken; they were broken all over. That was all I could see, his head and his hands, and I didn't want to open his clothing. I had to look away. It was the worst beating I had ever seen. I wanted to bring him up here, you know, but he couldn't get up and I was afraid to move him. I got a blanket and covered him, and then I went out and called an ambulance. Pretty soon it came, and they put him on a stretcher. He couldn't talk to them, and they told me I had to come along.

The rest of the night I waited around down there at the hospital. There were lots of doctors and nurses hurrying all around, and they wouldn't tell me anything, and I thought maybe he was dead or going to die, and I was just sitting there waiting, not knowing where he was or what was happening to him. After a while it got light outside, and one of the nurses came up to me and started asking me a lot of questions. They were silly questions, all about his family and his medical record and insurance and everything like that. I didn't know how to answer most of them, and I kept trying to get her to tell me how he was. She just went on, like those questions were the most important thing of all and acting like maybe I wasn't telling her the truth. She said they were going to have to file a police report, and she wanted to know exactly what had happened, and did he have any relatives who could come right away. And finally she said he was unconscious, and the doctor didn't know yet if he was going to be all right. She said it would be quite a long time before I could see him, and I told her I would wait. I guess she could see that I was pretty worried, and after a while she brought me a cup of coffee. Later, I remembered about going to work, and I called in and told Daniels that I was sick. He said O.K.

I waited all day. Late that afternoon they took me up to his room. It was dark in there and he was lying on his back asleep. They had cleaned him up pretty well and his head and arms and chest were all bandaged. They said I could sit in there by the bed if I wanted to. They had done about all they could, I guess, and everything seemed to be all right for the time being. Every once in a while a nurse would come in and look at him. He didn't wake up, and finally they told me I had to go home.

That night I called that white woman; I don't know why, but I figured I ought to do it. I didn't want Milly to know what had happened, and I couldn't think of anybody else to call. I guess I got all mixed up on the phone. She didn't know what I was talking about at first, and she kept asking me who I was and why I was calling her. I said I hoped she didn't mind me bothering her like that, but he was hurt pretty bad and I didn't know what else to do. She got real quiet for a minute, like she was thinking about it, you know, and then she thanked me and hung up. And two days later she came to the hospital.

I had been there for a while. He was awake and he could open one of his eyes, but his face was partly bandaged and it was hard for him to talk. I was going on about everything, you know, like it was going to be all right; that's when I made up those plans. Pretty soon she came into the room, and I knew right away who she was. She was all dressed up and good-looking and you could smell the perfume she had on. I was kind of embarrassed and I didn't know what to do and I got up to leave. But she said it was all right and please don't go, and she came over and shook my hand and thanked me again. My being there didn't seem to bother her at all, and right away she started talking to him. She said she was sorry he was sick, and she was sure he would be well again soon. She went on talking kind of fast, like she knew just what she wanted to say. I felt funny being there, but she didn't seem to mind, and she started telling him about her son, Peter. Peter was growing up, she said, and she had wanted to bring him along, but Peter was busy with his friends and couldn't come. She said that she had thought about *him* a lot and wondered how he was and what he was doing, you know, and she always thought kindly of him and he would always be her friend. Peter always asked her about the Indians, she said, and she used to tell him a story about a young Indian brave. He was born of a bear and a maiden, she said, and he was noble and wise. He had many adventures, and he became a great leader and saved his people. It was the story Peter liked best of all, and she always thought of *him*, Abel, when she told it. It was real nice the way she said it, like she thought a whole lot of him, and I could tell that story was kind of secret and important to her, you know, and it made me kind of ashamed to be there listening. She said she was awfully glad that I had called her, because she wouldn't have missed seeing him again for the world. I was glad that she had come, and I guess he was, too, but he didn't ever say anything about it afterward. I couldn't tell what he was thinking. He had turned his head away, like maybe the pain was coming back, you know.

Ei yei! A bear! A bear and a maiden. And she was a white woman and she thought it up, you know, made it up out of her own mind, and it was like that old grandfather talking to me, telling me about *Esdzá shash nadle,* or *Dzil quigi,* yes, just like that. How was it? I remember, yes; you drink a little wine and you remember. A long time ago it was dark, and you looked in the fire and listened, and he was going on with his work and talking, going on about all he knew, and he knew everything and there was no end to the stories and the songs.

And after those things happened, the people came down from the mesas. And they were afraid of *Esdzá shash nadle.* They buried the Calendar Stone and wrapped blankets made of feathers around their dead; they ran away, leaving their possessions. And there on the rock where they lived, they left the likeness of a bear.

Grandson, it was here, here at Kin tqel that they killed two of the cave people. There were twelve brothers and two sisters. It was time for the sisters to marry. And there were two old men, the Bear and the Snake. They went to the top of a mountain and bathed themselves. They put on fine clothes and were changed into men; they became young men, strong and good-looking. They smoked pipes, and the smoke was sweet, and it rolled down the mountain. The sisters came upon the trail of sweet smoke and were enchanted, and they climbed after it to the source. "Where do you come from?" the elder sister asked. "I came from the mountain," said the Bear. "And I came from the plain," said the Snake. The sisters drew smoke from the pipes and fell asleep. And when they awoke they knew that they had lain with a bear and a snake, and they were afraid. They ran away, the elder sister to the summit and the younger to the plain. The elder sister came at last to the great kiva of the Yeí bichai. Four holy men and four holy women came out to greet her. The women bathed and anointed her; they touched her with corn meal and pollen, and she was beautiful. She bore a female child. There were tufts of hair in back of its ears and down on its arms and legs. And then the Yei told the people to sing the Mountain Chant, and from that time on the elder sister was called the Bear Maiden.

Afterward a male child was born, and the Bear Maiden left it alone. The child cried, and an owl heard it and carried it away. The child grew and became strong. He was going to be a hunter, and the owl was afraid and meant to kill him. But the wind spoke to the child and told him to run away; he must follow the Río Mancos to the east.

He came of age and married the elder daughter of a great chief, and he was then a medicine man. But the younger daughter was beautiful, and he thought about her. He lay with her and she did not know who he was. But then she knew. She was going to bear a child and was ashamed. And when the child was born she hid it among the leaves. The child was found by the Bear.

> With beauty before me,
> With beauty behind me,
> With beauty above me,
> With beauty below me,
> With beauty all around me . . .

It's dark and rainy up there on the hill, and last night it was cool and clear. We went off by ourselves, you know, and we could hear the singing and see the stars. It's funny, but we didn't want to turn around. We knew the lights were there, all the rows and squares of light far below, and it was beautiful. I guess we knew without looking that it was great and beautiful, that everything was there, and beyond there was nothing but the black water and the sky. But we didn't want to turn around. We could hear the singing and see the stars. There was a faint yellow glare like smoke on the

sky, but the sky was too much for it, and at the center
we could see the stars, how small and still they were.
And he was going home.

I prayed. He was going home, and I wanted to pray.
Look out for me, I said; look out each day and listen
for me. And we were going together on horses to the
hills. We were going to ride out in the first light to the
hills. We were going to see how it was, and always was,
how the sun came up with a little wind and the light
ran out upon the land. We were going to get drunk, I
said. We were going to be all alone, and we were going
to get drunk and sing. We were going to sing about the
way it always was. And it was going to be right and
beautiful. It was going to be the last time. And he was
going home.

4

THE
DAWN RUNNER

Walatowa, 1952

FEBRUARY 27

The river was dark and swift, and there were jagged panes of ice along the banks, encrusted with snow. The valley was gray and cold; the mountains were dark and dim on the sky, and a great, gray motionless cloud of snow and mist lay out in the depth of the canyon. The fields were bare and colorless, and the gray tangle of branches rose up out of the orchards like antlers and bones. The town lay huddled in the late winter noon, the upper walls and vigas were stained with water, and thin black columns of smoke rose above the roofs, swelled, and hung out against the low ceiling of the sky. The streets were empty, and here and there were drifts of hard and brittle snow about the fence posts and the stones, pocked with soil and cinders. There was no telling of the sun, save for the one cold, dim, and even light that lay on every corner of the land and made no shadow, and the silence was close by and all around and the bell made no impression upon it. There was no motion to be seen but the single brief burst and billow of the smoke. And out of the town on the old road southward the snow lay unbroken, sloping up on either side to the rocks and the junipers and the dunes. A huge old jack rabbit bounded across the hillside in a blur of great sudden angles and settled away in the snow, still and invisible.

Father Olguin was at home in the rectory. He was alone and busy in the dark rooms, and in seven years he had grown calm with duty and design. The once-hectic fire of his spirit had burned low, and with it the waste of motion and despair. He had aged. He thought of himself not as happy (for he looked down on that particular abstraction) but in some real sense composed and at peace. In the only way possible, perhaps, he had come to terms with the town, and that, after all, had been his aim. To be sure, there was the matter of some old and final cleavage, of certain exclusion, the whole and subtle politics of estrangement, but that was easily put aside, and only now and then was it borne by a cold and sudden gust among his ordinary thoughts. It was irrelevant to his central point of view, nothing more than the fair price of his safe and sacred solitude. That safety—that exclusive silence—was the sense of all his vows, certainly; it had been brought about by his own design, *his* act of renunciation, not the town's. He had done well by the town, after all. He had set an example of piety, and much in the way of good works had accrued to his account. Once in a great while he took down from a high hidden shelf the dusty journal of Fray Nicolás. He regarded it now with ease and familiar respect, a kind of solemn good will. It lay open in his hands like a rare and wounded bird, more beautiful than broken, and with it he performed the mild spiritual exercise that always restored him to faith and humility.

Abel sat in the dark of his grandfather's house. Evening was coming on, and the bare gray light had begun to fail at the window. He had been there all day with his head hanging down in the darkness, getting up only to tend the fire and look in the old man's face. And he had been there the day before, and the day before that. He had been there a part of every day since his return. He had gone out on the first and second days and got drunk. He wanted to go out on the third, but he had no money and it was bitter cold and he was sick and in pain. He had been there six days at dawn, listening to his grandfather's voice. He heard it now, but it had no meaning. The random words fell together and made no sense.

The old man Francisco was dying. He had shivered all morning and complained of the cold, though there was a fire in the room and he lay under three blankets and Abel's gray coat. At noon he had fallen into a coma again, as he had yesterday and the day before. He revived in the dawn, and he knew who Abel was, and he talked and sang. But each day his voice had grown weaker, until now it was scarcely audible and the words fell together and made no sense: "*Abelito . . . kethá ahme . . . Mariano . . . frío . . . se dió por . . . mucho, mucho frío . . . vencido . . . aye, Porcingula . . . que blanco, Abelito . . . diablo blanco . . . Sawish . . . Sawish . . . y el hombre negro . . . sí . . . muchos hombres negros . . . corriendo, corriendo . . . frío . . . rápidamente . . . Abelito, Vidalito , . . ayempah? Ayempah!*"

Abel waited, listening. He tried to think of what to do. He wanted earlier, in the dawn, to speak to his grandfather, but he could think of nothing to say. He listened to the feeble voice that rose out of the darkness, and he waited helplessly. His mind was borne upon the dying words, but they carried him nowhere. His own sickness had settled into despair. He had been sick a long time. His eyes burned and his body throbbed and he could not think what to do. The room enclosed him, as it always had, as if the small dark

interior, in which this voice and other voices rose and
remained forever at the walls, were all of infinity that
he had ever known. It was the room in which he was
born, in which his mother and his brother died. Just
then, and for moments and hours and days, he had no
memory of being outside of it.

The voice was thin and the words ran together and
were no longer words. The fire was going out. He got
up and struck a match to the lamp. The white walls
moved in upon him, and the objects in the room stood
out; shadows leaped out upon the white walls, and the
windows were suddenly black and opaque, terminal as
mirrors to the sight. His body ached even with the
motion of getting up and crossing the room, and he
knelt down to place wood on the fire. He waited until
the wood caught fire and he could see the slender
pointed flames curling around the wood, and the wood
began to crackle and the bright embers flew against the
black earthen corner of the box and out upon the
hearth. Then the farther walls began faintly to glow and
vibrate with ripples of yellow light, and the firelight fell
and writhed upon the bed and the old man's face and
hair. And the old man's breathing was rapid and deep.
The vague shape of his body rose and fell, and the
voice rattled on, farther and farther away, and the eyes
darted and roved.

Abel smoothed the coat and drew it up to his grandfather's throat. The old man's face was burning, and his
lips were cracked and parched. Abel dipped a cloth in
water and pressed it gently to his grandfather's mouth.
He wanted to sponge the eyes, but they were open and
roving and straining to see, and he laid it on the brow
instead. There was nothing more to do, and he sat
down again at the table and hung his head. The walls
quivered around him and the fire began to hum and
roar and a thin steam grew up on the cold black
windows. There was a dull glint upon the empty bottles
that stood on the table, and, through the glass, a distortion of lines upon the ancient oilcloth. The kerosene
was low in the green glass well of the lamp, and now

and then the merest black wisp of smoke rose out of the globe. It was growing late, and he dozed. Still he could hear the faintest edge of his grandfather's voice on the deep and distant breathing out of sight, going on and on toward the dawn . . . another—one more dawn. The voice had failed each day, only to rise up again in the dawn. The old man had spoken six times in the dawn, and the voice of his memory was whole and clear and growing like the dawn.

They were old enough then, and he took his grandsons out at first light to the old Campo Santo, south and west of the Middle. He made them stand just there, above the point of the low white rock, facing east. They could see the black mesa looming on the first light, and he told them there was the house of the sun. They must learn the whole contour of the black mesa. They must know it as they knew the shape of their hands, always and by heart. The sun rose up on the black mesa at a different place each day. It began there, at a point on the central slope, standing still for the solstice, and ranged all the days southward across the rise and fall of the long plateau, drawing closer by the measure of mornings and moons to the lee, and back again. They must know the long journey of the sun on the black mesa, how it rode in the seasons and the years, and they must live according to the sun appearing, for only then could they reckon where they were, where all things were, in time. There, at the rounder knoll, it was time to plant corn; and there, where the highest plane fell away, that was the day of the rooster race, six days ahead of the black bull running and the little horse dancing, seven ahead of the Pecos immigration; and there, and there, and there, the secret dances, every four days of fasting in the kiva, the moon good for hoeing and the time for harvest, the rabbit and witch hunts, all the proper days of the clans and societies; and just there at the saddle, where the sky was lower and brighter than elsewhere on the high black land, the

*clearing of the ditches in advance of the spring rains
and the long race of the black men at dawn.*

These things he told to his grandsons carefully, slowly and at length, because they were old and true, and
they could be lost forever as easily as one generation is
lost to the next, as easily as one old man might lose his
voice, having spoken not enough or not at all. But his
grandsons knew already; not the names or the strict
position of the sun each day in relation to its house, but
the larger motion and meaning of the great organic
calendar itself, the emergency of dawn and dusk, summer and winter, the very cycle of the sun and of all the
suns that were and were to come. And he knew they
knew, and he took them with him to the fields and they
cut open the earth and touched the corn and ate sweet
melons in the sun.

He was a young man, and he rode out on the buckskin colt to the north and west, leading the hunting
horse, across the river and beyond the white cliffs and
the plain, beyond the hills and the mesas, the canyons
and the caves. And once, where the horses could not go
because the face of the rock was almost vertical and
unbroken and the ancient handholds were worn away
to shadows in the centuries of wind and rain, he
climbed among the walls and pinnacles of rock, adher-
ing like a vine to the face of the rock, pressing with no
force at all his whole mind and weight upon the sheer
ascent, running the roots of his weight into invisible
hollows and cracks, and he heard the whistle and moan
of the wind among the crags, like ancient voices, and
saw the horses far below in the sunlit gorge. And there
were the caves. He came suddenly upon a narrow ledge
and stood before the mouth of a cave. It was sealed
with silver webs, and he brushed them away. He bent
to enter and knelt down on the floor. It was dark and
cool and close inside, and smelled of damp earth and
dead and ancient fires, as if centuries ago the air had
entered and stood still behind the web. The dead embers and ashes lay still in a mound upon the floor, and

*the floor was deep and packed with clay and glazed
with the blood of animals. The chiseled dome was low
and encrusted with smoke, and the one round wall was
a perfect radius of rock and plaster. Here and there
were earthen bowls, one very large, chipped and broken
only at the mouth, deep and fired within. It was beautiful and thin-shelled and fragile-looking, but he struck
the nails of his hand against it, and it rang like metal.
There was a black metate by the door, the coarse,
igneous grain of the shallow bowl forever bleached with
meal, and in the ashes of the fire were several ears and
cobs of corn, each no bigger than his thumb, charred
and brittle, but whole and hard as wood. And there
among the things of the dead he listened in the stillness
all around and heard only the lowing of the wind . . .
and then the plummet and rush of a great swooping
bird—out of the corner of his eye he saw the awful
shadow which hurtled across the light—and the clatter
of wings on the cliff, and the small, thin cry of a
rodent. And in the same instant the huge wings heaved
with calm, gathering up the dead weight, and rose
away.*

*All afternoon he rode on toward the summit of the
blue mountain, and at last he was high among the falls
and the steep timbered slopes. The sun fell behind the
land above him and the dusk grew up among the trees,
and still he went on in the dying light, climbing up to
the top of the land. And all afternoon he had seen the
tracks of wild animals and heard the motion of the
dead leaves and the breaking of branches on either
side. Twice he had seen deer, motionless, watching,
standing away in easy range, blended with light and
shadow, fading away into the leaves and the land. He
let them be, but remembered where they were and how
they stood, reckoning well and instinctively their notion
of fear and flight, their age and weight.*

*He had seen the tracks of wolves and mountain lions
and the deep prints of a half-grown bear, and in the
last light he drew up in a small clearing and made his
camp. It was a good place, and he was lucky to have*

come upon it while he still could see. A dead tree had
fallen upon a bed of rock; it was clear of the damp
earth and the leaves, and the wood made an almost
smokeless fire. The timber all around was thick, and it
held the light and the sound of the fire within the
clearing. He tethered the horses there in the open, as
close to the fire as he could, and opened the blanket
roll and ate. He slept sitting against the saddle, and
kept the fire going and the rifle cocked across his
waist.

He awoke startled to the stiffening of the horses.
They stood quivering and taut with their heads high
and turned around upon the dark and nearest wall of
trees. He could see the whites of their eyes and the ears
laid back upon the bristling manes and the almost
imperceptible shiver and bunch of their haunches to the
spine. And at the same time he saw the dark shape
sauntering among the trees, and then the others, sitting
all around, motionless, the short pointed ears and the
soft shining eyes, almost kindly and discreet, the gaze
of the gray heads bidding only welcome and wild good
will. And he was young and it was the first time he had
come among them and he brought the rifle up and
made no sound. He swung the sights slowly around
from one to another of the still, shadowy shapes, but
they made no sign except to cock their heads a notch,
sitting still and away in the darkness like a litter of
pups, full of shyness and wonder and delight. He was
hard on the track of the bear; it was somewhere close
by in the night, and it knew of him, had been ahead of
him for hours in the afternoon and evening, holding the
same methodical pace, unhurried, certain of where it
was and where he was and of every step of the way
between, keeping always and barely out of sight, almost
out of hearing. And it was there now, off in the blackness, standing still and invisible, waiting. And he did
not want to break the stillness of the night, for it was
holy and profound; it was rest and restoration, the
hunter's offering of death and the sad watch of the
hunted, waiting somewhere away in the cold darkness

*and breathing easily of its life, brooding around at last
to forgiveness and consent; the silence was essential to
them both, and it lay out like a bond between them,
ancient and inviolable. He could neither take nor give
any advantage of cowardice where no cowardice was,
and he laid the rifle down. He spoke low to the horses
and soothed them. He drew fresh wood upon the fire
and the gray shapes crept away to the edge of the light,
and in the morning they were gone.*

*It was gray before the dawn and there was a thin
frost on the leaves, and he saddled up and started out
again, slowly, after the track and into the wind. At
sunrise he came upon the ridge of the mountain. For
hours he followed the ridge, and he could see for miles
across the land. It was late in the autumn and clear,
and the great shining slopes, green and blue, rose out of
the shadows on either side, and the sunlit groves of
aspen shone bright with clusters of yellow leaves and
thin white lines of bark, and far below in the deep folds
of the land he could see the tops of the black pines
swaying. At midmorning he was low in a saddle of the
ridge, and he came upon a huge outcrop of rock and
the track was lost. An ancient watercourse fell away
like a flight of stairs to the left, the falls broad and
shallow at first, but ever more narrow and deep farther
down. He tied the horses and started down the rock on
foot, using the rifle to balance himself. He went slowly, quietly down until he came to a deep open funnel in
the rock. The ground on either side sloped sharply
down to a broad ravine and the edge of the timber
beyond, and he saw the scored earth where the bear
had left the rock and gone sliding down, and the swath
in the brush of the ravine. He thought of going the
same way; it would be quick and easy, and he was
close to the kill, closing in and growing restless. But he
must make no sound of hurry. The bear knew he was
coming, knew better than he how close he was, was
even now watching him from the wood, waiting, but
still he must make no sound of hurry. The walls of the
funnel were deep and smooth, and they converged at*

the bank of the ravine some twenty feet below, and the ravine was filled with sweet clover and paintbrush and sage. He held the rifle out as far as he could reach and let it go; it fell upon a stand of tall sweet clover with scarcely any sound, and the dull stock shone and the long barrel glinted among the curving green and yellow stalks. He let himself down into the funnel, little by little, supported only by the tension of his strength against the walls. The going was hard and slow, and near the end his arms and legs began to shake, but he was young and strong and he dropped from the point of the rock to the sand below and took up the rifle and went on, not hurrying but going only as fast as the bear had gone, going even in the bear's tracks, across the ravine and up the embankment and through the trees, unwary now, sensible only of closing in, going on and looking down at the tracks.

And when at last he looked up, the timber stood around a pool of light, and the bear was standing still and small at the far side of the brake, careless, unheeding. He brought the rifle up, and the bear raised and turned its head and made no sign of fear. It was small and black in the deep shade and dappled with light, its body turned three-quarters away and standing perfectly still, and the flat head and the small black eyes that were fixed upon him hung around upon the shoulder and under the hump of the spine. The bear was young and heavy with tallow, and the underside of the body and the backs of its short, thick legs were tufted with winter hair, longer and lighter than the rest, and dull as dust. His hand tightened on the stock and the rifle bucked and the sharp report rang upon the walls and carried out upon the slopes, and he heard the sudden scattering of birds overhead and saw the darting shadows all around. The bullet slammed into the flesh and jarred the whole black body once, but the head remained motionless and the eyes level upon him. Then, and for one instant only, there was a sad and meaningless haste. The bear turned away and lumbered, though not with fear, not with any hurt, but haste,

slightly reflexive, a single step, or two, or three, and it
was overcome. It shuddered and looked around again
and fell.

The hunt was over, and only then could he hurry; it
was over and well done. The wound was small and
clean, behind the foreleg and low on the body, where
the fur and flesh were thin, and there was no blood at
the mouth. He took out his pouch of pollen and made
yellow streaks above the bear's eyes. It was almost
noon, and he hurried. He disemboweled the bear and
laid the flesh open with splints so that the blood
should not run into the fur and stain the hide. He ate
quickly of the bear's liver, taking it with him, thinking
what he must do, remembering now his descent upon
the rock and the whole lay of the land, all the angles of
his vision from the ridge. He went quickly, a quarter of
a mile or more down the ravine, until he came to a
place where the horses could keep their footing on the
near side of the ridge. The blood of the bear was on
him, and the bear's liver was warm and wet in his
hand. He came upon the ridge and the colt grew wild in
its eyes and blew, pulling away, and its hoofs clattered
on the rock and the skin crawled at the roots of its
mane. He approached it slowly, talking to it, and took
hold of the reins. The hunting horse watched, full of
age and indifference, switching its tail. There was no
time to lose. He held hard to the reins, turning down
the bit in the colt's mouth, and his voice rose a little
and was edged. Slowly he brought the bear's flesh up
to the flaring nostrils of the colt and smeared the
muzzle with it.

And he rode the colt back down the mountain, leading the hunting horse with the bear on its back, and,
like the old hunting horse and the young black bear, he
and the colt had come of age and were hunters, too. He
made camp that night far down in the peneplain and
saw the stars and heard the coyotes away by the river.
And in the early morning he rode into the town. He
was a man then, and smeared with the blood of a bear.
He shouted, and the men came out to meet him. They

came with rifles, and he gave them strips of the bear's
flesh, which they wrapped around the barrels of their
guns. And soon the women came with switches, and
they spoke to the bear and laid the switches to its hide.
The men and women were jubilant and all around, and
he rode stone-faced in their midst, looking straight
ahead.

She was the child of a witch. She was wild like her
mother, that old Pecos woman whom he feared, whom
everyone feared because she had long white hair about
her mouth and she hated them and kept to herself. But
the girl was young and beautiful, and her name was
Porcingula. The women of the town talked about her
behind her back, but she only laughed; she had her
way with their sons, and her eyes blazed and gave them
back their scorn.

It was a warm summer night, and she waited for him
by the river. He came upon the sand in the cut of the
bank and did not see her. He stood looking around and
called her name. There was no answer, and the river
ran in the moonlight and the leaves of the cottonwood
were still and black against the sky. And at last she
came out of hiding, laughing and full of the devil.
"Well, you were early after all," she said, "and Mariano
had not done with me." "Come," he said, and he took
her breasts in his hands and moved against her and
kissed her mouth. But first she must have her way,
playful and mocking. Was he not a sacristan now?
Francisco was his name, and had he not been sired by
the old consumptive priest? Had he not been told by
his father who she was? So she went on, would go on
for a while, keeping him on a string, but he stroked her
body and she grew quiet and supple with hunger. And
she drew him down upon the sand and placed his
hands on her naked flesh, the warm curve of her belly
and the long dark hollows of her thighs, pressing the
tips of his fingers to the tendons and the angle of the
hair, into the hot wet flesh that sucked open and
closed and quickened to his touch. And then she was

wild and on fire and she opened her thighs and he came
upon her suddenly and hard and deep, and she writhed
under him, pleading and cursing and catching at her
breath, and she made small hard hooks of her hands
and heels and set them with all her strength into his
shoulders and his back, holding the awful swerve of his
force down and upon her, into the buck of her loins.

She laughed and wept and carried his child through
the winter, and as her time drew near she became more
and more beautiful. The wild brittle shine fell away
from her eyes and the hard high laughter from her
voice, and her eyes were sad and lovely and deep, and
she was whole and small and given up to him. But he
was wary; the women of the town whispered among
themselves, and the old priest hid away and stared at
his back. And sometimes in the night, when she lay
close beside him, he thought of who she was and turned
away. The child was stillborn, and she saw that the
sight of it made him afraid, and it was over. The shine
came again upon her eyes, and she threw herself away
and laughed.

"Abelito! Ándale, muchacho!"
He would go soon to the fields, but first there was
something he must do, and he sent Vidal ahead in the
wagon. He put his younger grandson in front of him
on the horse and they rode out a little way north from
the town. They crossed the broad Arroyo Bajo which
ran south and east from Vallecitos and came to the
cinch of the valley. There in the plain, between the blue
hills and the low line of the red cliffs, was the round red
rock. As they approached it from the south, it seemed
only a grade, a gentle rise in the plain, but when they
came upon it the land fell away. He took the boy down
from the horse, and they stood on the edge of the rock,
facing north, and the deep red face of the rock dropped
under them forty feet to the plain. The near fields lay
out below, and they could see across a hundred hills to
the mouth of the canyon. "Listen," he said, and they
stood perfectly still on the edge of the rock. The sun

took hold of the valley, and the morning breeze rose out of the shadows and the long black line of the eastern mesa backed away. Far below, the breeze ran upon the shining blades of corn, and they heard the footsteps running. It was faint at first and far away, but it rose and drew near, steadily, a hundred men running, two hundred, three, not fast, but running easily and forever, the one sound of a hundred men running. "Listen," he said. "It is the race of the dead, and it happens here."

It was November. The long line of wagons lay out on the road, and there was a low roar of fires and voices on the town. All morning the sky had been gray, and the gray haze of the smoke lay still above the roofs, and pale squadrons of geese flew south on the river. But at noon the smoke rose away and the sky cleared. Then the weather was clear and cold, and a sudden burst of colors came out upon the land. The walls deepened into gold and the fires ran into the glowing earth and the sun struck fire upon the scarlet pods that bled from the vigas. The squash clan came from the kiva, and he with them, standing apart with the drum. The dancers took their places, and he waited; it seemed a long time before they were ready, and he waited. He had never carried the drum before, and he was self-conscious and afraid. The old men, the singers and officials, would watch him, were watching him now. He wore white pants and a borrowed silver belt. The queue of his hair was wrapped around with a bright new cloth, and there was a rust-colored rouge under his eyes. He tried to think ahead to the songs, to all the dips and turns of the dancers, the rattle of the gourds, to all the measured breaks in the breath and the skipping beat of the drum, but it all ran together in his mind, and he waited under the eyes of the elders, fidgeting and full of dread. The chant began low and away, and the two dancers at the heads of the lines moved out, and one after another the others followed, so that a perfect chain of motion ran slowly upon the lines from front to back and the lines drew slowly out and sound swelled upon them. The

drum rolled like thunder in his hand, and he had no
memory of setting the deep sound upon it. It had
happened, and he no longer had fear, not even any
thought of fear. He was mindless in the wake of the
dancers, riding high like the gourds on the long bright
parallels of motion. He had no need of seeing, nor did
the dancers dance to the drum. Their feet fell upon the
earth and his hand struck thunder to the drum, and it
was the same thing, one motion made of sound. He lost
track of the time. An old man came beside him with
another drum, larger and warm from the fire. He
waited, going on, not counting, having no fear and
waiting for the pass, only nodding to the beat. And the
moment came in mid-motion, and he crossed the stick to
the heated drum and the heavy heated drum was in his
hand and the old man turned—and nothing was lost,
nothing; there had been nothing of time lost, no miss in
the motion or the mind, only the certain strange fall of
the pitch, the deeper swell of the sound on the warm
taut head of the drum. It was perfect. And when it was
over, the women of the town came out with baskets of
food. They went among the singers and the crowd,
throwing out the food in celebration of his perfect act.
And from then on he had a voice in the clan, and the
next year he healed a child who had been sick from
birth.

There was a moment in which he knew he could not
go on. He had begun at the wrong pace, another and
better man's pace, had seen the man come almost at
once to the top of his strength, hitting his stride without
effort, unlimbering and lining out and away. And like a
fool he had taken up the bait, whole and at once, had
allowed himself to be run into the ground. In the next
instant his lungs should burst, for now they were burning with pain and the pain had crowded out the last
and least element of his breath, and he should stum-
ble and fall. But the moment passed. The moment
passed, and the next and the next, and he was running

still, and he could see the dark shape of the man running away in the swirling mist, like a motionless shadow. And he held on to the shadow and ran beyond his pain.

FEBRUARY 28

Abel was suddenly awake, wide awake and listening. The lamp had gone out. Nothing had awakened him. There was no sound in the room. He sat bolt upright, staring into the corner where his grandfather lay. There was a deep red glow on the embers, and the soft light opened and closed upon the walls. There was no wind outside, nor any sound; only a thin chill had come in from the night and it lay like the cold of a cave on the earthen floor. He could see no movement, and he knew that the old man was dead. He looked around at the windowpanes, those coal-black squares of dim reflection. There was nothing. It was a while still before the dawn, before the first light should break in advance of the seventh dawn, and he got up and began to get ready. There was no need for the singers to come; it made no difference, and he knew what had to be done. He drew the old man's head erect and laid water to the hair. He fashioned the long white hair in a queue and wound it around with yarn. He dressed the body in bright ceremonial colors: the old man's wine velveteen shirt, white trousers, and low moccasins, soft and white with kaolin. From the rafters he took down the pouches of pollen and of meal, the sacred feathers and the ledger book. These, together with ears of colored corn, he placed at his grandfather's side after he had sprinkled meal in the four directions. He wrapped the body in a blanket.

It was pitch black before the dawn, and he went out along the corrals and through the orchards to the mission. The motor turned and, one after another, the lights went on upstairs and in the stair well and in the hall, and Father Olguin threw open the door.

"What in God's name—?" he said.

"My grandfather is dead," Abel said. "You must bury him."

"Dead? Oh . . . yes—yes, of course. But, *good heavens,* couldn't you have waited until—"

"My grandfather is dead," Abel repeated. His voice was low and even. There was no emotion, nothing.

"Yes, yes. I heard you," said the priest, rubbing his good eye. "Good Lord, what time is it, anyway? Do you know what *time* it is? I can understand how you must feel, but—"

But Abel was gone. Father Olguin shivered with cold and peered out into the darkness. "I can understand," he said. "I understand, do you hear?" And he began to shout. "I understand! *Oh God! I understand—I understand!*"

Abel did not return to his grandfather's house. He walked hurriedly southward along the edge of the. town. At the last house he paused and took off his shirt. His body was numb and ached with cold, and he knelt at the mouth of the oven. He reached inside and placed his hands in the frozen crust and rubbed his arms and chest with ashes. And he got up and went on hurriedly to the road and south on the wagon road in the darkness. There was no sound but his own quick, even steps on the hard crust of the snow, and he went on, and on, far out on the road.

The pale light grew upon the land, and it was only a trick of the darkness at first, the slow stirring and standing away of the night; and then the murky, leaden swell of light upon the snow and the dunes and the black evergreen spires. And the last deepened into light above the black highland, soft and milky and streaked with gray. He was almost there, and he saw the runners standing away in the distance.

He came among them, and they huddled in the cold together, waiting, and the pale light before the dawn rose up in the valley. A single cloud lay over the world, heavy and still. It lay out upon the black mesa, smudging out the margin and spilling over the lee. But at the saddle there was nothing. There was only the clear pool of eternity. They held their eyes upon it, waiting, and, too slow and various to see, the void began to deepen and to change: pumice, and pearl, and mother-of-pearl, and the pale and brilliant blush of orange and of rose. And then the deep hanging rim ran with fire and the sudden cold flare of the dawn struck upon the arc, and the runners sprang away.

The soft and sudden sound of their going, swift and breaking away all at once, startled him, and he began to run after them. He was running, and his body cracked open with pain, and he was running on. He was running and there was no reason to run but the running itself and the land and the dawn appearing. The sun rose up in the saddle and shone in shafts upon the road across the snow-covered valley and the hills, and the chill of the night fell away and it began to rain. He saw the slim black bodies of the runners in the distance, gliding away without sound through the slanting light and the rain. He was running and a cold sweat broke out upon him and his breath heaved with the pain of running. His legs buckled and he fell in the snow. The rain fell around him in the snow and he saw his broken hands, how the rain made streaks upon them and dripped soot upon the snow. And he got up and ran on. He was alone and running on. All of his being was concentrated in the sheer motion of running on, and he was past caring about the pain. Pure exhaustion laid hold of his mind, and he could see at last without having to think. He could see the canyon and the mountains and the sky. He could see the rain and the river and the fields beyond. He could see the dark hills at dawn. He was running, and under his breath he began to sing. There was no sound, and he had no voice; he had only the words of a song. And he went running on the rise of the song. *House made of pollen, house made of dawn. Qtsedaba.*

About the Author

N. Scott Momaday, a Kiowa Indian, spent his childhood on Indian reservations in the Southwest. He is currently Professor of English at Stanford University in California. He is also the author of *The Gourd Dancer* (poems), *The Way to Rainy Mountain* (folk tales), and *The Names* (an autobiography). He is married and the father of three daughters.